Diseases & Disorders

Mood Disorders

Titles in the Diseases and Disorders series include:

Acne
AIDS
Alzheimer's Disease
Anorexia and Bulimia
Anthrax
Arthritis
Asthma
Attention Deficit Disorder
Autism
Bipolar Disorder
Birth Defects
Breast Cancer
Cerebral Palsy
Chronic Fatigue Syndrome
Cystic Fibrosis
Deafness
Diabetes
Down Syndrome
Dyslexia
Epilepsy
Fetal Alcohol Syndrome
Food Poisoning
Growth Disorders
Headaches
Heart Disease
Hemophilia
Hepatitis
Human Papillomavirus (HPV)
Leukemia
Lou Gehrig's Disease
Lyme Disease
Mad Cow Disease
Malaria
Malnutrition
Measles and Rubella
Meningitis
Mental Retardation
Multiple Sclerosis
Obesity
Ovarian Cancer
Parkinson's Disease
Phobias
SARS
Schizophrenia
Sexually Transmitted Diseases
Sleep Disorders
Smallpox
Strokes
Teen Depression
Toxic Shock Syndrome
Tuberculosis
West Nile Virus

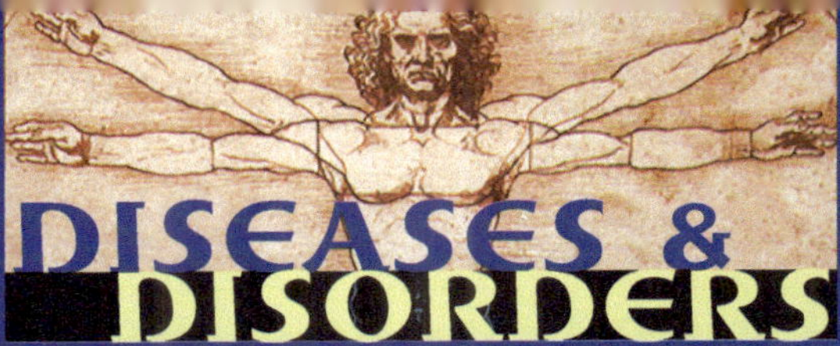

DISEASES & DISORDERS

Mood Disorders

Lizabeth Peak

LUCENT PRESS

Published in 2008 by
Lucent Press, an Imprint of Greenhaven Publishing, LLC
353 3rd Avenue
Suite 255
New York, NY 10010

LIBRARY OF CONGRESS CATALOGING-IN-PUBLICATION DATA

Peak, Lizabeth.
Mood disorders / by Lizabeth Peak.
p. cm. -- (Diseases & disorders)
Includes bibliographical references and index.
ISBN 978-1-4205-0072-1 (hardcover)
1. Affective disorders--Juvenile literature. 2. Depression, Mental--Juvenile literature. I. Title.
RC537.P424 2008
616.85'27--dc22

2008004173

Some of the images in this book illustrate individuals who are models. The depictions do not imply actual situations or events.

CPSIA compliance information: Batch #BW08KL: For further information contact Greenhaven Publishing LLC, New York, New York, at 1-844-317-7404.

Please visit our website, www.greenhavenpublishing.com. For a free color catalog of all our high-quality books, call toll free 1-844-317-7404 or fax 1-844-317-7405.

Printed in the United States of America
1 2 3 4 5 6 7 12 11 10 09 08

Table of Contents

Foreword 6

Introduction
An Exploding Epidemic 8

Chapter 1
What Are Mood Disorders? 14

Chapter 2
Types of Mood Disorders 31

Chapter 3
Diagnosis and Treatment 49

Chapter 4
Living with Mood Disorders 65

Chapter 5
On the Horizon 82

Notes 97

Glossary 101

Organizations to Contact 106

For More Information 108

Index 111

Picture Credits 119

About the Author 120

FOREWORD

"The Most Difficult Puzzles Ever Devised"

Charles Best, one of the pioneers in the search for a cure for diabetes, once explained what intrigued him so about medical research: "It's not just the gratification of knowing one is helping people," he confided, "although that probably is a more heroic and selfless motivation. Those feelings may enter in, but truly, what I find best is the feeling of going toe to toe with nature, of trying to solve the most difficult puzzles ever devised. The answers are there somewhere, those keys that will solve the puzzle and make the patient well. But how will those keys be found?"

Since the dawn of civilization, nothing has so puzzled people—and often frightened them, as well—as the onset of illness in a body or mind that seemed healthy before. Being unable to reverse conditions such as a seizure, the inability of a heart to pump, or the sudden deterioration of muscle tone in a small child, or even to understand why they occur was unspeakably frustrating to healers. Even before there were names for such conditions, before they were understood at all, each was a reminder of how complex the human body was and how vulnerable.

While our grappling with understanding diseases has been frustrating at times, it has also provided some of humankind's most heroic accomplishments. Alexander Fleming's accidental discovery in 1928 of a mold that could be turned into penicillin has resulted in the saving of untold millions of lives. The isolation of the enzyme insulin has reversed what was once a death sentence for anyone with diabetes. There also have been great strides in combating conditions for which there is not yet a cure. Medicines can help AIDS patients live longer, diagnostic tools such as mammography and ultrasounds can help doctors find tumors while they are treatable, and laser surgery techniques have made the most intricate, minute operations routine.

This "toe-to-toe" competition with diseases and disorders is even more remarkable when viewed in a historical continuum. An astonishing amount of progress has been made in a very short time. Just two hundred years ago, the existence of germs as a cause of some diseases was unknown. In fact, less than 150 years ago a British surgeon named Joseph Lister had difficulty persuading his fellow doctors that washing their hands before delivering a baby might increase the chances of a healthy delivery (especially if they had just attended to a diseased patient)!

Each book in Lucent's Diseases and Disorders series explores a disease or disorder and the knowledge that has been accumulated (or discarded) by doctors through the years. Each book also examines the tools used for pinpointing a diagnosis, as well as the various means that are used to treat or cure a disease. Finally, new ideas are presented—techniques or medicines that may be on the horizon.

Frustration and disappointment are still part of medicine because not every disease or condition can be cured or prevented. But the limitations of knowledge are constantly being pushed outward; the "most difficult puzzles ever devised" are finding challengers every day.

INTRODUCTION

An Exploding Epidemic

Peggy had always considered herself an upbeat, joyful person with lots to live for. Married for thirty years, she was a successful writer, salesperson, mother, and grandmother. Then, in 1985, her life began to unravel. "I used to work at a bank," says Peggy, "and I can remember not being able to add two plus two and get four. It was like my brain was in a fog and would not work properly. I handled it by simply getting through it, and ended up being off work for three months."[1] Over the next eleven years, her problems grew. Peggy lost all of her energy. There were nights when she could not sleep, and days when she could not get out of bed. In the summer of 1997 Peggy found herself in the hospital with chest pain. She began to have hot flashes and night sweats. Her doctors told her she was going through menopause, the condition women experience as their reproductive years end. It got so bad, however, that Peggy considered suicide. "It was like I was in this huge black hole," she notes, "and there was no life and no hope."[2] Fortunately for Peggy, she eventually found a doctor who recognized her symptoms and diagnosed her with depression.

A Common, and Still Growing, Problem

Depression is one of a group of mental illnesses called mood disorders, sometimes referred to as affective disorders. In addition to depression, mood disorders include such illnesses as bipolar disorder (formerly called manic depression), seasonal affective disorder (SAD), and postpartum depression. Mood

In some people a symptom of depression, a common mood disorder, may be the inability to get out of bed on a daily basis.

disorders affect a person's emotional state, or mood, and can include a wide variety of symptoms. The same disorder can look different in different people. A teenage girl cannot get out of bed after breaking up with her boyfriend. A thirty-year-old woman becomes depressed and isolates herself from family and friends, but only from late fall until early spring. A new mother cries all the time and wishes she had never had her baby. A young man paints his entire apartment red, overnight, and then considers suicide the next day. All of these people are suffering from different types of mood disorders.

According to the National Institute of Mental Health (NIMH), almost 10 percent of Americans over the age of eighteen—about twenty million people—struggle with some type of mood disorder. A 1999 report from the U.S. surgeon general stated that mood disorders rank among the top ten causes of disability worldwide, with major depression ranking number one and bipolar disorder at number six. More Americans suffer from mood disorders than from AIDS, cancer, and heart disease combined, and the incidence of mood disorders continues to increase, for several reasons. First, today's fast-paced, achievement-oriented society places a great deal of stress on people, which can seriously affect one's emotional state. Second, greater geographic mobility means that family members are more separated from one another, and family ties and the emotional support that comes with them are strained. Third, as the social stigma of having a mood disorder decreases, more people with symptoms are willing to seek professional help. Lastly, increased understanding and knowledge about mood disorders means they are more often being diagnosed correctly.

Mood disorders do not discriminate. They can affect anyone of any age, race, or sex. The average age of onset for most mood disorders is in the early to mid-twenties, but in the 1980s mental health professionals began to recognize the symptoms in teens and even young children. It is estimated that between 7 and 14 percent of children will experience at least one episode of major depression by the time they turn fifteen. According to the Center for Mental Health Services, about 2.5 million Americans under the age of eighteen and one in every ten teenagers suffer from clinical depression. Rates of depression are especially high among sixteen- and seventeen-year-olds. Twenty to thirty percent of adults with bipolar disorder say they had their first episode before they turned twenty. Because symptoms are often explained away as "typical" teenage behavior, less than half receive treatment.

Older adults may also suffer from depressive illnesses. Depression is not a normal part of aging, but it can be more difficult to recognize in the elderly because symptoms of depression are often mistaken for other age-related illnesses such as Alzheimer's disease. Research has shown that rates of depression are higher among the elderly who live in nursing homes than among those who live in a community.

Both men and women are affected by mood disorders, but women are about twice as likely to experience a mood disorder at some time in their lives. This is especially true for depression. While depression is equally as common in younger boys and girls, when girls begin having menstrual periods, their risk for depression significantly increases.

Because mood disorders can strike anyone at any time, the effect on family and relationships cannot be overlooked. "When someone you love is depressed," says one doctor, "you may live with a chronic sense of uncertainty, never really knowing when your loved one will recover from a depressive episode or fall into a new one. You can feel profound loss—even grief and anger—that life has deviated, maybe permanently, from the norm."[3]

A Billion-dollar Problem

Mood disorders also have a significant impact on the nation's economy. According to Mental Health America, a nonprofit organization dedicated to mental health issues, depression alone costs U.S. businesses at least $44 billion a year in absenteeism, lost productivity, and treatment costs. Researchers at Harvard Medical School put that figure at closer to $50 billion. A study done in 2006 by the NIMH showed that each U.S. worker with bipolar disorder missed an average of 65.5 workdays in one year, and workers with major depression averaged 27.2 lost workdays per year, for a total of more than 300 million lost workdays.

Even in light of these facts, many employers are reluctant to address the emotional needs of their employees and are not comfortable talking about them. Many insurance plans do not pay for mental illness treatment or may cover only very limited services. "That's not the kind of treatment any other illness gets," says Ellyn Jaeger of Mental Health America of Georgia. "That's not adequate. Businesses, if they want a healthy work force, need to realize how serious depression is."[4]

A social stigma is still attached to mood disorders. Many people who suffer from them spend thousands of dollars on unnecessary tests and therapies, hoping to find a more socially acceptable explanation for their symptoms, while the actual cause may go undiagnosed for years. At the same time, mood disorders are often associated with other mental and physical

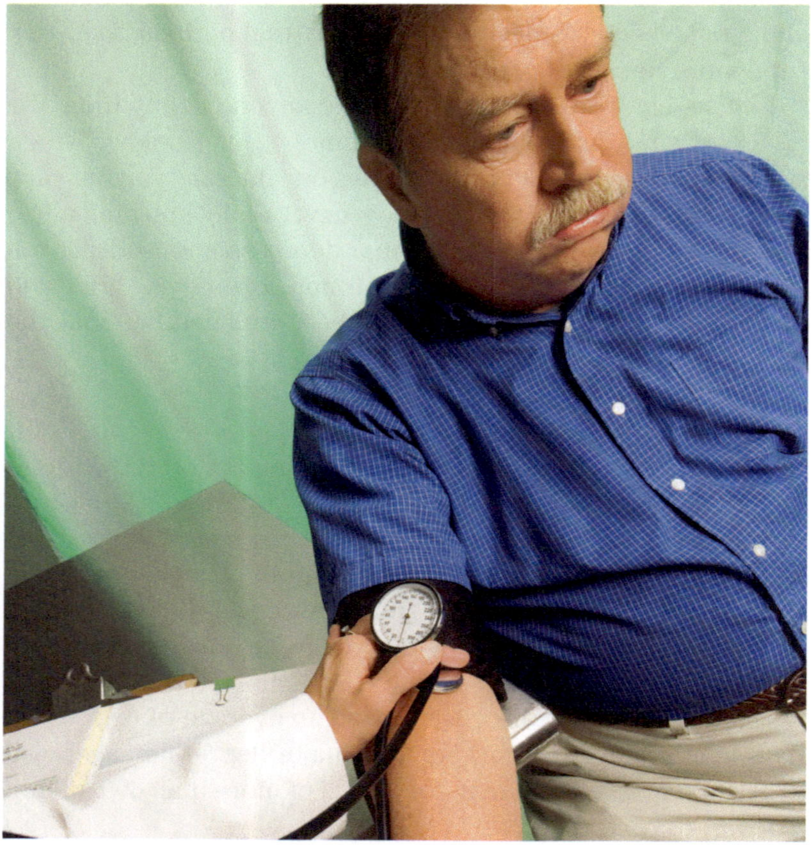

Physical problems, such as high blood pressure and arthritis, are often associated with mood disorders and lead to increased doctor visits to deal with these ailments.

ailments such as high blood pressure, arthritis, and substance abuse, leading to increased doctor visits for these problems. A 1998 study estimated that the average lifetime health care cost for a person with bipolar disorder ranged from about $11,700 for treatment of a single manic episode to almost $625,000 for a long-term illness. The study estimated the total lifetime cost for the treatment of all people in the United States with bipolar disorder to be approximately $24 billion. Another study reported $7 billion in costs not related to treatment, such as an increased use of the criminal justice system. At the individual and family level, the loss of income from absent employment, missed workdays, and the high cost of therapy and medications places financial and emotional stress on the family coping with a mood disorder.

A Much Brighter Outlook

Until fairly recently, people with mood disorders and other mental illnesses were subjected to negative societal stereotypes. They were called weak or lazy and were told to just "snap out of it." Today, people with mood disorders and their families are educated about their illness and can take an active part in treatment. Many sources of help and support are available, and new therapies are continually being developed. Along with greater understanding has come increased acceptance of mood disorders and the people who have them.

CHAPTER ONE

What Are Mood Disorders?

At some time or another everyone feels sad. Loss of a loved one, long-term illness, personal or professional rejection, and any of a host of other events can trigger feelings of sadness, loneliness, or isolation. Some people may react to these events with anger, irritability, or hostility. These are normal reactions to stressful events in life. When the feelings do not go away, however, when they have no apparent cause, or when they prompt major changes or disruptions in a person's life, there may be a problem that requires attention. Someone struggling with these feelings and reactions may have a mood disorder.

Mood disorders are illnesses, just like diabetes, asthma, or cancer. People suffering from mood disorders have at times been characterized as lazy, misbehaving, or having a bad attitude. These are misconceptions, or mistaken beliefs. People with mood disorders require treatment and support similar to the needs of any patient dealing with a long-term, recurrent illness.

Mood disorders are a category of mental health problems that include all forms of depression and bipolar disorders. Depression causes lasting and sometimes overwhelming feelings of sadness, worthlessness, and hopelessness. Bipolar disorders involve wild mood swings from deep depression to episodes of mania, or being overly "high." Both depression and bipolar disorder can be life-threatening, and suicide is a very

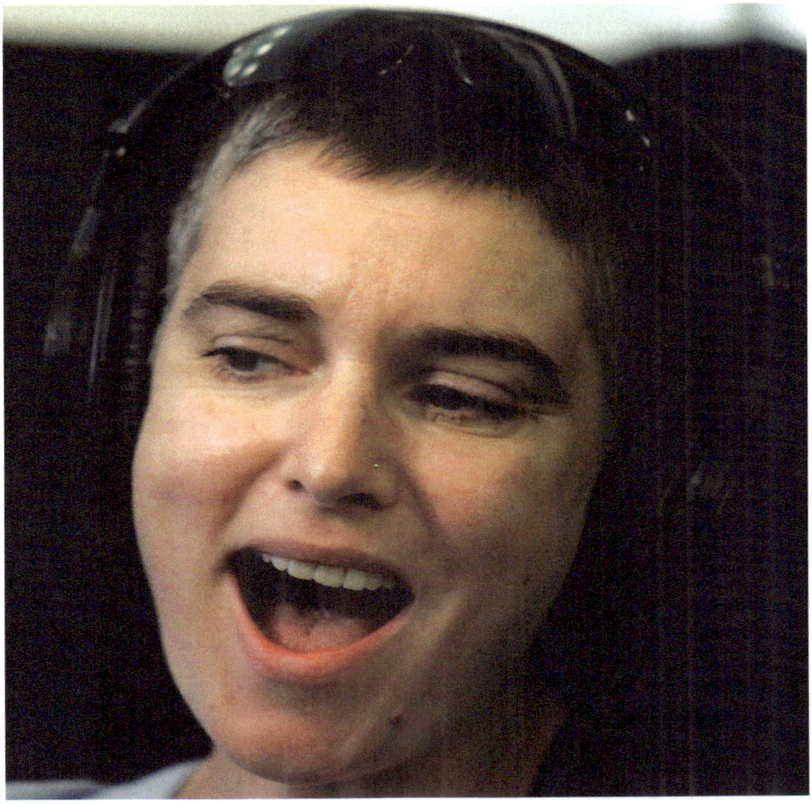

Before being diagnosed and receiving treatment for the mood disorder known as bipolar disorder, singer Sinead O'Connor often struggled with thoughts of suicide.

real possibility with both types of disorders. Mood disorders are usually episodic, meaning that the symptoms come and go with periods of feeling "normal" in between. The episodes may vary in duration—how long the mood lasts, or in intensity—how strongly the emotion is felt. Mood disorders, therefore, are basically disturbances in both a person's emotions and mood.

Emotions

An emotion is a complex state of feeling that happens automatically in response to events that are meaningful to the person in some way. Human beings have the ability to experience dozens of different emotions. They include such feelings as anger, happiness, love, hate, grief, hopefulness, fear, confidence, jealousy, and disgust.

Emotions are complex because they have several components, or parts, to them. The psychological, also called experiential, part is what the person experiences in his mind, or the way the emotion feels. The experience can be positive and good, as when a person feels happy or excited. It can also be negative and unpleasant, as when a person feels sad, angry, or afraid.

The behavioral component of emotions is shown in the way the person acts, or behaves, in response to the emotion. A simple example of this is facial expression. Emotions often show in the faces a person makes, which changes as his emotions change. It is usually not difficult to tell what a person is feeling by looking at his expression. Some expressions are common to all human beings. For example, no matter where in the world they live, all people frown when they are angry and smile when they are happy. Other behaviors may also be triggered by emotions. Anger may cause a person to shout at or strike another person. Fear may cause a person to run away. Love may make a person want to give a hug to the loved one.

The physiological, or somatic, component is what happens in the body physically when a person experiences an emotion. Different emotions can trigger the release of certain chemicals in the brain that affect physical processes in the body. For example, when a person feels afraid, his heart rate and blood pressure may increase. Anxiety may cause stomach pain, sleeplessness, or headaches. Happiness make a person feel relaxed and can lower blood pressure.

Mood

The other aspect of mood disorders is mood itself. The word "mood" refers to a prolonged state of emotion or a combination of emotions that can affect the way a person views the world around him. It is the way a person feels inside, and it may last a few hours or it may go on for years. Because it is more

If a person's emotions frequently swing between very "down" and very "up," it may be a sign that the person has a mood disorder.

long-lasting than emotion, a person's mood often becomes quite apparent to the people around him, and it can affect his relationships with others at work or school, and even his physical health. While everyone experiences fluctuations, or up-and-down changes in their mood, a problem may be developing if the fluctuations frequently swing from one extreme to the other, from very "up" to very "down," or if the mood seems to be stuck at one of the extremes for a long time.

Causes of Mood Disorders

Emotion and mood are very subjective concepts. This means that each person responds to life events in his or her own way, depending on that person's individual personality and learned ways of reacting to things. An emotional response that may be "normal" for one person and may be very unusual for another. The subjective nature of emotion and mood can make it difficult to understand where mood disorders come from and what causes them.

Researchers have several theories about what causes mood disorders. They include biological, genetic, and environmental factors as well as stressful lifetime events. Most often, what causes a mood disorder in any individual is a combination of factors, and the particular combination is different for different people. While no one is completely safe from developing a mood disorder, some groups of individuals seem to be more at risk for developing one than others. Certain features of these groups that are associated with mood disorders are called risk factors.

Risk Factors for Mood Disorders

One of the most important risk factors for developing a mood disorder, especially depression, is gender. In the United States, women are twice as likely as men to develop depression and are more likely to seek treatment for it. In childhood, both boys and girls are about equally likely to have a depressive type of mood disorder, but as they approach adolescence, girls tend to become depressed more often than boys. This continues into

A Long History

Mood disorders and other mental illnesses have been known since the beginnings of recorded history. People who behaved in strange, unexplained ways were called "lunatics" or "maniacs." Sufferers were often banished from society, tortured, or even killed. Thousands were condemned to suffer and die in lunatic asylums, sometimes called "snake pits" because of their terrible conditions. Mental illnesses were often thought to be the result of supernatural evil forces, possession by the devil, punishment for sin, or witchcraft. The ancient Greeks offered more scientific, physiological explanations. The ancient physician Hippocrates (460?–370? B.C.) believed that abnormal behavior was caused by imbalances in the various fluids, or "humors," in the body. An early word for depression, melancholia, literally means "black bile." Mentally ill people were treated with such extreme measures as trephination, in which a hole is drilled into the person's skull to let the evil out, or by exorcism, a religious practice for banishing evil spirits. It was not until the late 1800s that doctors began to study and describe mental illness as a distinct category, and the field of modern psychology, or study of the mind, was born.

A patient tethered to the wall in the Bedlam Lunatic Asylum in 1814. During the 1800s people with mental illnesses were often mistreated and banished from society.

adulthood; about 25 percent of women, compared to about 12 percent of men, will experience at least one episode of major depression in their lifetime.

There are several possible reasons for this difference. One is that women may tend to be more willing than men to seek treatment. Women on the whole tend to be more accepting of the kinds of feelings that go along with depression and are not as reluctant to admit their feelings and share them with others. Men are more likely to keep their feelings private, or they may mask their symptoms with the use of alcohol or other substances. In some ways, women in American society may be under more stress than men. Many women juggle the demands of home, children, careers, and other roles that result in more responsibilities for them. In addition, women's hormone lev-

American women are twice as likely as American men to develop depression. This may be due to the demands now placed on women with work, home, and children.

els shift frequently due to monthly menstrual cycles, pregnancy, childbirth, and menopause and these may play a role in depression.

Age may also be a factor in the development of depression. Most mood disorders begin roughly between the ages of twenty and thirty, but older people may be at particular risk as they face late-life issues such as chronic health problems, the loss of friends, distancing of family members, retirement, and decreased income. "Empty nest syndrome" is a common occurrence in which adults, especially women, whose children have grown and moved away, face life without the parenting role that defined and filled their lives for so many years. Men who retire after being in the workforce for decades may feel useless and empty without the "family provider" role that they occupied for so long.

Heredity and Mood Disorders

Heredity is another significant risk factor for mood disorders. The genes that people inherit from their parents determine most of the characteristics they will have, such as gender, height, or eye color. Genes also determine what diseases or illnesses a person may be vulnerable to getting. It is known that people who have one or more close relatives with depression or bipolar disorder may be as much as three times more likely than those with no affected relatives to become depressed themselves. Siblings and children of those with bipolar disorder are eight to ten times more likely to develop the condition. Relatives of bipolar patients are also more likely to develop major depressive illness than the general population; about 50 percent of bipolar patients have at least one parent with major depression.

Much information about the heredity of depression has come from studying twins, because they have identical genes (or genetic codes) in their DNA. Research has shown that if one twin becomes depressed, the other will also become depressed about 76 percent of the time. Even if they are raised apart from each other, they will both become depressed 67 percent of the time. In fraternal, or nonidentical, twins, the rate of both twins becoming depressed is much lower, but it is still higher than siblings who are not twins.

Pinpointing the Problem

In spring 2007 scientists at Stanford University School of Medicine published a two-part study that looked at 650 families in which at least two family members suffered from repeated episodes of severe depression. In the first part, the researchers examined the entire group of genes—the genome—of each family member, looking for particular genetic characteristics, or "markers," that are linked with depression. The second part of the study took a closer look at the most suspicious area, located on chromosome 15, which had a total of 103 such markers. A chromosome is a piece of genetic material, or DNA. "We found highly significant evidence for linkage to depression in this particular part of chromosome 15," said Dr. Douglas Levinson, director of the study. "This finding has a very good chance of leading to the discovery of a gene that could yield important information about why some people develop depression."[5]

Researchers have found evidence that depression may be linked to a particular chromosome, like the one pictured here.

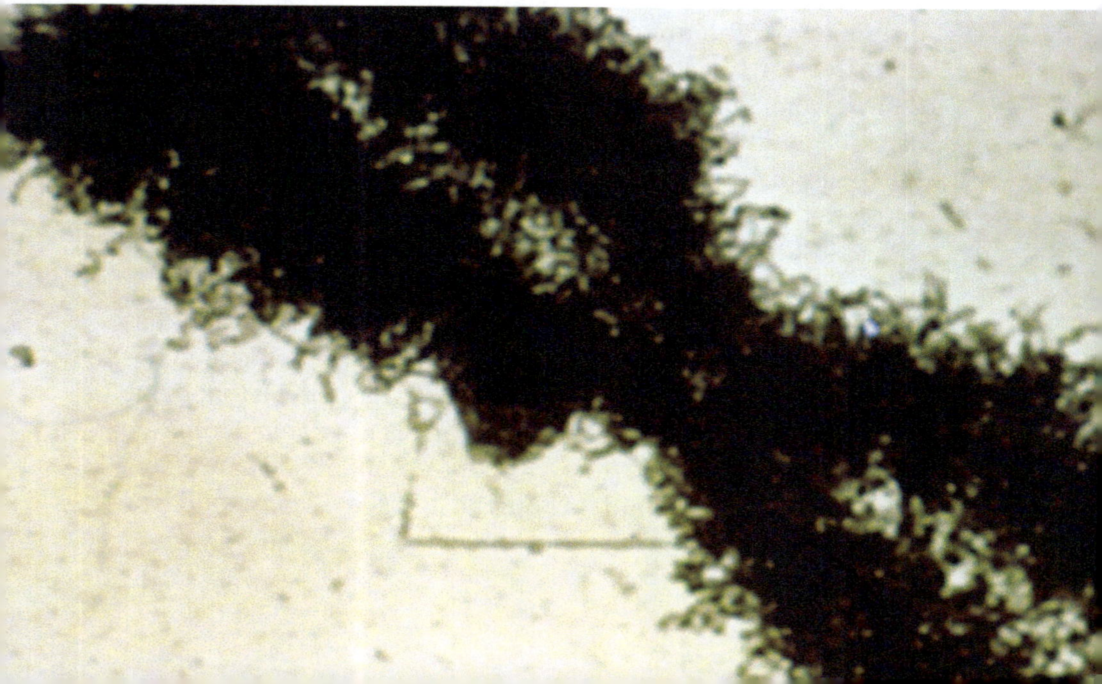

Inheriting a gene for depression or bipolar disorder does not mean a person will definitely develop it. The fact that identical twins, who have the exact same genes, do not always both become depressed suggests that there are other biological factors that can make a person vulnerable to developing a mood disorder.

The Brain and Mood Disorders

Biological causes of mood disorders have to do with physical events within the body that have an effect on mood, emotion, and stress, and on how a person responds to them. Biological causes are mainly concerned with one major organ—the brain.

The brain is like the command center of the human body. It controls all of the biological processes that support life, including thought, mood, and emotion. Many researchers now believe that mood disorders, as well as many other forms of mental illness, are caused by imbalances of certain chemicals, called neurotransmitters, in the brain. The portion of the brain in which these neurotransmitters work and that has the most influence over human emotion is called the limbic system.

The Limbic System—The Center of Emotions

The limbic system is a rather complex set of structures near the center of the brain that controls emotional responses, especially fear, aggression, and pleasure. It also has an important role in the formation and storage of memories. One of the busiest parts of the limbic system is the hypothalamus, which sits deep inside the brain. The hypothalamus receives lots of information about what is going on in the body from many different sources, such as nerves and other parts of the brain. In response to this information, it sends out instructions to the rest of the body, mainly through two ways. It influences the endocrine system, which is responsible for regulating the various hormones in the body. Adrenalin, the so-called "fight or flight" hormone, is controlled in this way. The hypothalamus also affects the autonomic nervous system, the part of the nervous system that controls body functions such as heart rate, sweating, and blood pressure. This function of the hypothalamus explains why strong emotion can make people sweat and feel as if their hearts are "racing."

Another very active part of the limbic system is the amygdala, a small, almond-shaped structure that is the center for fear and aggression. When this part of the brain is stimulated in lab animals, they become aggressive. If the amygdala is removed, the animals no longer respond to things that would have caused fear or aggression before. The amygdala is linked to a third structure in the limbic system called the hippocampus.

The hippocampus, located inside the temporal lobes of the brain, on either side of the head near the temples, is responsible for making and storing new memories. Memory and emotion are very closely related. This is demonstrated every time a person thinks of a memory and feels again the emotion that he felt when the event first occurred. Many of our most vivid memories are associated with strong emotion, especially fear and anger.

Neurotransmitters

The structures in the limbic system transfer their messages using special chemicals in the brain called neurotransmitters. Neurotransmitters act as chemical messengers in the brain. They allow electrical impulses in the brain to be transferred from one neuron, or nerve cell, to the next, until the message arrives at its intended place. When an electrical impulse reaches the end of one neuron, it gets converted into a chemical—the neurotransmitter—which carries the impulse across the space between the neurons, called the synapse, to special receptor sites on the next neuron. This process happens at a very high rate of speed—less than 1/5000th of a second. This is what allows us to react so quickly to stimuli such as fear or pain. In people with mood disorders, this normally efficient process seems to go wrong. The receiving neuron may be either too sensitive or not sensitive enough to its neurotransmitter, or the sending neuron may produce too little of the neurotransmitter so that the message does not get sent properly. Any problem

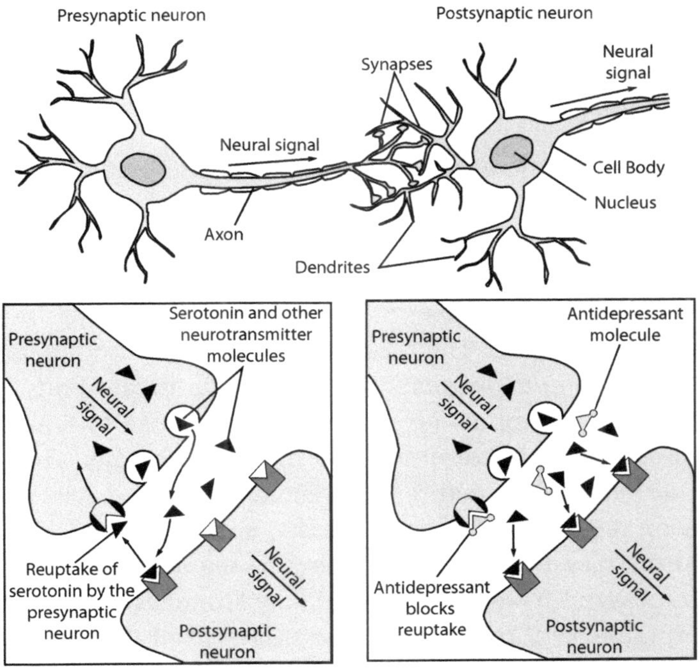

An illustration of a neuron producing a neurotransmitter. In people with mood disorders, the production of neurotransmitters may not work correctly.

with this very finely tuned process can cause a disturbance in mood.

As of the mid-2000s approximately thirty different kinds of neurotransmitters have been identified. Three of these are particularly associated with mood disorders: serotonin, norepinephrine, and dopamine. They function within the parts of the brain responsible for emotion, stress reactions, sleep, appetite, blood pressure, and sexuality. It is not entirely clear how these chemicals are related to a person's mood. Some people who are depressed have a lower than normal level of norepinephrine, but other depressed people have a higher than normal level. Some severely depressed people have very low levels of serotonin. Dopamine levels seem to fall during periods of depression and rise during episodes of mania. Some medications can lower dopamine levels, and depression can be a side effect of these drugs.

Endorphins

Another kind of neurotransmitter in the brain that affect mood are called endorphins. Endorphins are produced in the hypothalamus. They are sometimes called the body's natural pain killers because their chemical structure resembles drugs such as morphine and because they can reduce pain and create a sense of well-being. The word "endorphin" is a combination of the words *endogenous*, meaning "made in the body," and *morphine*. Endorphins are released in response to fear, pain, or other physical stress such as intense exercise. This may explain how acupuncture, the ancient Chinese practice of applying needles to the body, works, and why people in emotional distress may deliberately injure themselves by cutting. These otherwise painful activities may stimulate the release of endorphins. Endorphins may also be released during pleasurable activities such as laughing, eating sweets, listening to soft music, or lying in the sun.

Hormones and Emotion

Another possible biological cause for disorders of mood has to do with the endocrine system. The endocrine system is composed of several small organs called glands, located throughout the body. Examples of endocrine glands include the thyroid, the adrenal glands, the pancreas, the ovaries in girls, and the testes in boys. Endocrine glands secrete hormones into the bloodstream. Each endocrine gland produces its own special hormone. The hormones in the blood travel to their particular "target" organs, telling them what to do. For example, insulin from the pancreas allows the body's cells to use sugar for energy. In adolescence, testosterone from the testes tells a boy's hair follicles in his skin to start growing body hair and tells his muscles to start growing larger. Estrogen from the ovaries tells a girl's body to develop breasts and start having menstrual periods.

The activity of the endocrine glands is controlled by a special gland called the pituitary, located at the base of the brain. The pituitary gland is itself controlled by the hypothalamus, part of the limbic system in the brain. The hypothalamus uses the three neurotransmitters—serotonin, norepinephrine, and dopamine—to regulate the endocrine system. Because of the connections between the hypothalamus and the endocrine system, it is believed that problems in the endocrine system may be at least partly responsible for some of the common symp-

If the endocrine system is not working correctly, it may result in a person developing a mood disorder.

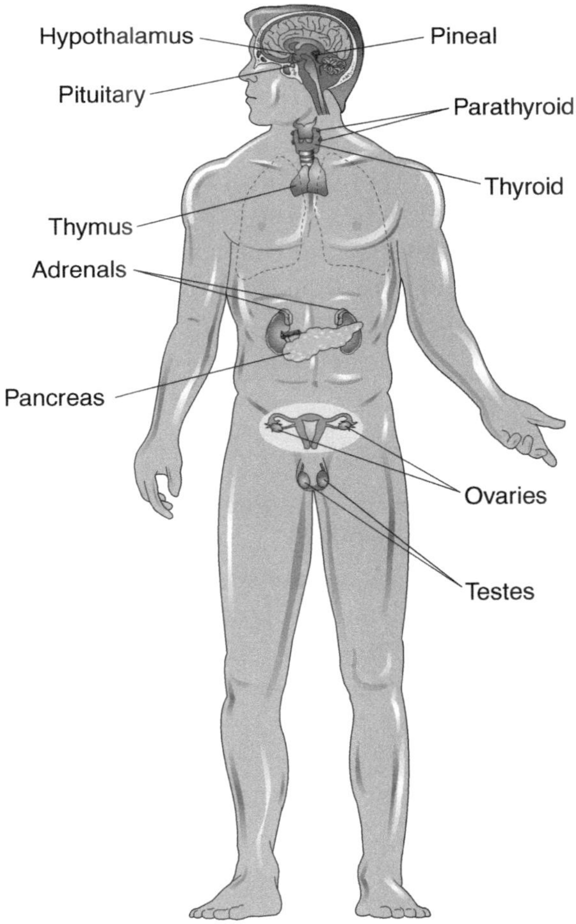

toms of depression, such as loss of appetite, sleeplessness, and decreased sex drive.

One particular hormone that has been connected with depression is cortisol. Cortisol is produced by the adrenal glands in response to stress. About half of people who are depressed have excess cortisol in their blood. Researchers believe that the problem may lie with the hypothalamus. If the hypothalamus does not monitor the levels of cortisol properly, it may send the wrong message to the pituitary, which in turn sends the wrong message to the adrenal glands. When depression is treated, high cortisol levels often return to more normal levels.

Environmental Causes of Mood Disorders

Biological factors causing mood disorders are concerned with what goes on inside the body. Environmental factors are concerned with what goes on outside the body, in the person's environment. They are not related to genetics or brain chemistry or hormones. Environmental causes are related to stressful events that take place in a person's life, such as stress at home or at work, loss of a loved one or of a close relationship, or a traumatic event such as being the victim of a crime. It is well known that a person's experiences have a direct effect on his or her emotions, thoughts, and behavior. The ways in which a person responds to stressful experiences may influence the development of a mood disorder, especially depression, in a vulnerable person.

Stress

Almost everyone is familiar with the uncomfortable feelings of stress. Most people, when they think of stressful events, remember unpleasant or difficult situations. Pressure to perform well in school or in sports, fear of failure, conflicts with others, or changes such as going through puberty or moving to a new place, can all cause a great deal of stress. Stress, however, can also be caused by more positive events, such as getting married, starting a new job, or taking an overseas vacation. Either type of event can cause stress that may lead to depression.

Laughter Really is the Best Medicine

Laughter not only improves mood, it may actually help protect people against a heart attack, according to a 2005 study by cardiologists at the University of Maryland Medical Center in Baltimore. "The old saying that 'laughter is the best medicine', definitely appears to be true when it comes to protecting your heart," said Michael Miller, M.D., director of the Center for Preventive Cardiology at the University of Maryland Medical Center and associate professor of medicine at the University of Maryland School of Medicine. "We don't know yet why laughing protects the heart, but we know that mental stress is associated with impairment of the endothelium, the protective barrier lining our blood vessels. This can cause a series of inflammatory reactions that lead to fat and cholesterol build-up in the coronary arteries and ultimately to a heart attack." Laughter is also known to release endorphins, the body's natural mood elevators, lower blood pressure, and lower levels of the stress hormone cortisol.

Quote from Michelle W. Murray, "Laughter is the Best Medicine for Your Heart," University of Maryland Medical Center, 2007, www.umm.edu/features/laughter.htm.

It is not fully understood whether a single stressful event can actually cause a person to become depressed. Some people may have several stressful experiences and never become depressed; others may become depressed when there is little or no apparent stress in their lives. When a single event does lead to a depressive episode, it is most likely to be a first or second episode. After that, episodes may seem to come on without a noticeable cause. Researchers call this the "kindling effect." Psychologist Dr. Prentiss Price, Ph.D. explains, "Initial depressive episodes spark changes in the brain's chemistry and limbic system that make it more prone to developing future episodes of depression. This may be compared to the use of kindling wood to spark the flames of a campfire. Since early episodes of depression make a person more sensitive to developing depression, even small stressors can lead to later depressive episodes."[6]

Both depression and bipolar disorders have similar risk factors and can be caused by similar types of biologic, genetic, and environmental factors. These two major types of mood disorders are very different from each other, however, with different symptoms.

Types of Mood Disorders

Mood disorders include symptoms that can fall anywhere along the range of moods and emotions, from one extreme to the other. At one end of the range are the symptoms of depression—extreme sadness, loss of energy, hopelessness, helplessness, and sometimes the desire to end one's own life. At the other end are the sometimes bizarre symptoms of mania, such as extreme elation, very high energy, talkativeness, sleeplessness, and feelings of invincibility and boundless ability.

Unipolar Versus Bipolar

Mood disorders fall into two very broad categories: unipolar depression and bipolar disorder. "Unipolar," meaning "one end," means that the symptoms tend to stay mainly at the low, or depressive, end. "Bipolar" means that the person's mood can swing wildly from one end, or pole, of the mood spectrum to the other, from depression to mania and back again, sometimes within hours of each other.

Depression or "The Blues"?

At the low end of the mood spectrum is depression. True depression is much more than just feeling sad or having "the blues." Without treatment, depression can last for weeks, months, or years. It can severely affect a person's ability to work, go to school, interact with friends and family, or even get out of bed

Depression is different than "the blues" because without treatment it may last for an extended period of time and affect a person's ability to work, go to school, and socialize.

in the morning. Eighteen-year-old Shannon describes how she felt after she and her boyfriend of one year broke up. "It's natural to be sad when you have a break-up. I've always been a moody kid. Feeling blue was nothing new to me. But this was different. I was so down. Weeks went by, and I couldn't get over it. All of a sudden I'd feel like crying. And then I couldn't stop sobbing. I wasn't sleeping or eating. I'd toss in bed at night.

When the morning came, I dreaded going to school."[7] Shannon had more than just "the blues." She was depressed.

True depression can lead to substance abuse, self-mutilating behavior such as cutting, or even suicide. Most mental health experts look for two major indicators—the duration of symptoms, or how long they last, and the intensity of symptoms, or how significantly they interfere with daily life. The most severe form of depression is called major depression.

Suicide

Suicide—the taking of one's own life—is probably the most extreme and the most tragic expression of depression. Without treatment, depressed people may become so overwhelmed with sadness and hopelessness that they can see no other way out. At that point, they are unable to think about anyone or anything else. Often, they do not actually want to die. They just want to stop the emotional pain that they feel every day.

Suicide is the third leading cause of death among teens and young adults. Nearly five thousand teens commit suicide each year. Half of all teens who commit suicide abuse drugs or alcohol. Since the 1980's the suicide rate for children age ten to fourteen has doubled.

Almost always, there are warning signs. Some signs that have been associated with suicide are: talking about it or threatening to do it; having a sudden change in personality or behavior; making preparations such as making a will or giving away belongings; buying a gun or other weapon; engaging in high-risk behavior such as driving too fast or running away from home; becoming involved with drugs or alcohol; withdrawing from friends and family; and sudden improvement in mood after being down for a long time.

When someone talks about suicide, it should always be taken seriously and never as if the person was trying to "get attention." Most communities have suicide hotlines to call when a person is feeling suicidal or when a friend or loved one shows warning signs. Hospitalization is sometimes necessary to protect the person from suicide.

Major Depression

The *Diagnostic and Statistical Manual of Mental Disorders*, fourth edition, text revision, (*DSM-IV-TR*) is a manual mental health professionals use to guide them in diagnosing all kinds of mental illnesses. The *DSM* defines major depression as feeling overwhelmingly sad or irritable, or both, almost all the time, and losing interest in people and activities that used to provide pleasure and enjoyment. These feelings last for most of the day, every day, for at least two weeks, and are associated with other symptoms such as insomnia or hypersomnia (oversleeping), changes in appetite with weight loss or gain, lack of energy, feelings of hopelessness and worthlessness, and possibly thoughts of suicide. In addition to the emotional symptoms, depressed people often have physical symptoms as well, such as headaches, stomachaches, or muscle and joint pain. To be true depression, the symptoms must not be caused by substance abuse or another medical illness or be side effects of a medication. They are noticeable to others or to the patient herself, and they cause significant problems at home, work, or school.

A major depressive episode, or the period of time during which a person is having symptoms, may occur only once in a person's life, but more commonly they occur several times in a lifetime. About 50 to 60 percent of people who have one episode of major depression will have a second one, and the chances of having an episode increase greatly with each episode. Although depression most often affects adult women, it can also affect men and people in other age groups.

Depression in Men

Although depression is much more common in women, it is estimated that about six million men in the United States suffer from it. For several reasons, depression appears quite different in men than in women, and it often goes unrecognized. From a young age, males are socialized to be strong, competitive, and successful. They are often reluctant to talk about how they feel emotionally. As a result, they are less likely to seek medical

Men are much more likely to mask their depression with the use of drugs or alcohol.

help for their symptoms, and they are more likely than women to mask their distress with overworking, drugs, or alcohol. Men who are depressed tend to become irritable, hostile, angry, or even violent, rather than hopeless, sad, or tearful. They are more likely than women to engage in reckless behavior. Bill, an attorney who struggles with depression, says, "When I was feeling depressed I was very reckless with my life. I didn't care about how I drove, I didn't care about walking across the street carefully, I didn't care about dangerous parts of the city. I wouldn't be affected by any kinds of warnings on travel or places to go. I didn't care whether I lived or died and so I was going to do whatever I wanted whenever I wanted. And when you take those kinds of chances, you have a greater likelihood of dying."[8]

One potentially devastating consequence of this is suicide. Although women are more likely than men to attempt suicide, men are about four times more likely than women to be successful at it. Of all people who commit suicide in the United States, 80 percent of them are men. One reason for this may be that men tend to use more lethal or violent methods, such as a gun or hanging, rather than taking a drug overdose as do many suicidal women.

Depression in the Elderly

For most adults over the age of sixty-five, life is fulfilling and happy, but for some it is a time of regret and sadness, with little hope for improvement. Physical ailments may interfere with an older adult's ability to participate in activities they used to enjoy. With advancing age, they may experience the loss of their former roles in the family and the workplace. With the loss of their spouse or having to move from their homes, important sources of social support are lost. Suicide is a real risk. The suicide rate for older people is 50 percent higher than for younger people. Each year, approximately 6,300 older adults commit suicide.

As in men, depression in the elderly is often overlooked. When older people show signs of depression, it is often dismissed as a normal part of growing old. In addition, the social stigma, or shame, about mental illness is felt strongly in older people, who may have been raised in a time when mood disorders were less understood, and they may be reluctant to talk to their doctor about their feelings. Depression-like symptoms in older adults may be attributed to other medical problems, such as thyroid disease, or they may be side effects of some medications frequently prescribed for older people. True depression, however, is not normal in any age group. Fortunately, with treatment, the later years can still be happy and satisfying for the depressed older person and her family.

Depression in Children and Teens

As with men and the elderly, depression in children and teens may be overlooked, for several reasons. Few people, including health professionals, expect children to be depressed, especially pre-teen children. Children may be unable to clearly describe what they are feeling, and they may express it in behavior rather than with words. They may misbehave at home or at school, pretend to be sick to avoid school, cling to a parent, or worry about things. Katherine, a fourteen-year-old with depression, remembers feeling overwhelmed with sadness early in her life. "Everyone always thought I was weird. I remember being picked on all the way back in fourth grade. It really got to me. I'd hurry home and turn off all the lights in my

Children with depression are often misdiagnosed because they cannot describe how they are feeling.

room and bury myself under the bed covers for hours. Soon I stopped doing my homework...Hey, what little kid doesn't get bummed out by teasing? Still, I began to see myself the way others did: I was weird."[9]

Teens often express depression with irritability or hostility rather than with profound sadness, and this may be passed off as just "being a teenager." Parents and teachers may assume that the child or teen is simply going through a "phase" that will eventually go away. If the parents seek medical help, the doctor may refer the child or teen to a psychologist or psychiatrist who specializes in children's mental health.

Major depression is the most common and most severe form of depression, but there are other forms that can have an equally profound effect on a person's life and the lives of those around them.

Dysthymia

Dysthymia is similar to major depression except that the symptoms are not as severe. As with other forms of depression, almost twice as many women as men develop dysthymia, and twin studies show that often both twins are affected. People with dysthymia tend to worry a lot and feel guilty about minor things. They may say that they feel gloomy or "down" all the time and that they have always felt that way. As a result, the diagnosis of dysthymia is often missed because the person believes that this is just the way she is.

Although not as overwhelming as major depression, the symptoms of dysthymia have a major impact on a person's life because they tend to last for a longer period of time—at least two years for adults and at least one year for children and adolescents. The symptoms may subside somewhat during that time, but the person is never symptom-free for more than two months at a time. There may also be periods of more severe major depressive symptoms during that time, a combination called "double depression." About 40 percent of people with dysthymic disorder also have major depression. They may

Types of Mood Disorders		
Name	**Type**	**Symptoms**
Major Depression	Unipolar	Insomnia or hypersomnia, weight loss or weight gain, lack of energy, feelings of hopelessness and worthlessness, and sometimes thoughts of suicide
Dysthymia	Unipolar	Tendency to worry and feel guilty about little things and a "gloomy" feeling all of the time
Seasonal Affective Disorder (SAD)	Unipolar	Symptoms usually occur during late autumn and winter, they are similar to major depression, and most people with SAD have an increased appetite, weight gain, and cravings for carbohydrates and sweets
Postpartum Depression	Unipolar	Irritability; trouble sleeping; crying spells; fear of being an inadequate mother; feelings of hopelessness, guilt, sadness, and anxiety; headaches, hyperventilation, and chest pain; indifference, resentment, or hostility towards the new infant; severe agitation; hallucinations; deep depression; confusion; and uncontrollable anger
Mania	Bipolar	Feelings of euphoria, extreme irritability, aggressiveness, hyperactivity, extreme energy, restlessness, trouble concentrating, fast talking, and sleeplessness
Hypomania	Bipolar	Periods of unusual creativity and energy and extreme good feeling

also have other disorders such as anxiety, phobias, substance abuse, or attention deficit hyperactivity disorder (ADHD).

Seasonal Affective Disorder (SAD)

Seasonal Affective Disorder (SAD) is a unique type of depression in which symptoms tend to show up only during certain times of the year, usually late autumn and winter. First described in 1984, it has also been called seasonal depression or winter depression. Women develop SAD two to four times more often than men. It is less common in people over age fifty, and it is rarely seen in people over sixty-five. SAD is more common in northern areas of the United States than in southern areas.

Most mental health professionals believe that SAD is caused by reduced exposure to sunlight in winter. Light affects the brain's production of the hormone melatonin, which is produced by the brain during periods of darkness. It regulates the body's circadian rhythm, the twenty-four-hour biological clock of sleep, body temperature, and hormone secretion. An overproduction of melatonin during winter's dark days and long nights may trigger depression in some people. Light may also affect the production of the neurotransmitters serotonin and dopamine.

SAD has four main features that define it. First, the depressive episodes of SAD begin and end at about the same time every year. Second, this pattern occurs at least two years in a row. Third, the person is free of symptoms for at least two months in a row during the rest of the year. Fourth, although the person may feel depressed at other times of the year, there are more episodes during the winter than any other season.

Symptoms of SAD are similar to those of major depression, but 70 to 90 percent of people with SAD also experience increased appetite, weight gain, and cravings for carbohydrates and sweets. Twenty percent may go on to develop bipolar disorder, with the manic episodes occurring during the spring and summer. This is what happened to Cathy, who says, "I feel my bipolar is extremely seasonal. In the spring and summer, I am more likely to be manic…, sleeping only three to five hours a night. In the fall and winter I am much more likely to be depressed and sluggish."[10]

Postpartum Depression

Another unique kind of depression is postpartum depression. The word "postpartum" means "after birth" and this kind of depression occurs shortly after a woman gives birth. It is common for many women to feel some mood swings after having a baby. It can be a very challenging time, especially for a first-time mother. This normal period of "baby blues" usually subsides after ten days to two weeks. Some women, however, experience a deeper and longer lasting depression. This is true postpartum depression.

Three different forms of postpartum depression have been described by researchers. The most minor form, similar to the baby blues, usually starts within a few days after delivery, and is characterized by irritability, sleep problems, crying spells, and feelings of helplessness and fear of being an inadequate mother. This form is fairly common; researchers estimate that as many as 80 percent of new mothers experience this form of postpartum depression.

The second form is somewhat more severe and consists of more intense feelings of helplessness, guilt, sadness, and anxiety. There may also be physical symptoms such as headaches,

Postpartum depression is a deep depression experienced by women who have recently given birth and lasts longer than the typical "baby blues."

hyperventilation, which is rapid breathing because of the inability to catch one's breath, and chest pain. The new mother may regard her infant with indifference, resentment, or hostility. This form occurs in about 10 percent of new mothers.

The least common but most severe form, postpartum psychosis, occurs in about one in a thousand births. It begins usually within four weeks of childbirth. Symptoms may include severe agitation, hallucinations, deep depression, confusion, and uncontrollable anger. The mother experiencing postpartum psychosis may be in danger of harming herself or her baby, and sometimes hospitalization is necessary in order to treat this extreme form of postpartum depression.

It is not clear what causes postpartum depression. It may be related to the rapid hormone changes that occur during and just after birth, which can have a major effect on emotions and mood. It may be triggered by the stress of giving birth and having the responsibility of caring for a newborn. It may be related to the age of the mother or the availability to her of help and support. It is known, however, that women who have experienced depression before pregnancy are at a higher risk for developing postpartum depression.

Bipolar Disorders

The other major class of mood disorders is bipolar disorder, formerly called manic depression. Bipolar disorder differs from unipolar depression in that it has two extremes of emotion and mood, rather than just one. People with bipolar disorder experience drastic mood swings, from severe highs, called mania, to the equally severe lows of depression. These shifts in mood are different from the normal ups and downs that all people experience from time to time. Sometimes these mood swings occur very suddenly, but more often they happen gradually.

Bipolar disorders are not as common as other depressive disorders, but they still affect more than two million Americans age eighteen and older. Symptoms usually begin in late adolescence or young adulthood, but they may also begin in childhood or in later years. A person at the depressive end of bipolar

"Baby Blues" for Dads?

Postpartum depression may not just be an illness for women. According to research reported in 2006, about 10 percent of new fathers also showed some symptoms of moderate or severe depression after the birth of their children. Research leader Dr. James F. Paulson of Eastern Virginia Medical School says, "The long-standing belief of many people, including physicians, has been that postpartum depression is due to hormone changes in women that take place after childbirth. Obviously, fathers wouldn't be susceptible to changes of this nature and, probably because of this, haven't been a focus of study." Other social, psychological, and stress factors, however, may also play a role in postpartum depression. "Factors of this nature certainly can affect fathers," says Dr. Paulson, "and they probably do in many families." Adds Janice Goodman, a psychiatric clinical nurse specialist, "In both men and women, the huge life changes that go along with having a baby can contribute to depression." She stresses the importance of checking on the health of fathers whose partners are experiencing signs of postpartum depression.

Quotes from "Postpartum Depression: A Risk for New Dads, Too," *HealthDay News*, June 8, 2007, http://www.healthday.com/Article.asp?AID=601383.

disorder shows symptoms very similar to unipolar depression. At the other end of the mood spectrum, however, are the often bizarre symptoms of mania.

Mania

As with depression, mania can severely interfere with a person's ability to function effectively at home, work, school, or in social situations. People in the manic phase of the bipolar cycle may appear euphoric, or in an abnormally good mood, or they may be extremely irritable, aggressive, and quick to anger. They may be hyperactive and have a great deal of energy.

Charlie Crow was diagnosed with bipolar disorder in 2001. According to a 2007 study, the number of children diagnosed with bipolar disorder has increased, but some experts question whether these children have been mislabeled.

They may be very restless and unable to sit or stand still for more than a few seconds. They may have trouble concentrating, jumping rapidly from one idea to the next, and talking very fast. This is called "flight of ideas," and it can be very difficult for anyone trying to talk with the person to keep up with or to understand their conversation. They may be unable to sleep, and they may be prone to abuse alcohol or drugs, especially sleep medications. Kate, a teen with bipolar disorder, describes her experience:

> The first time that I went through a manic period, I thought I was having the time of my life. I loved school and my grades were excellent. I was staying after school, helping with the yearbook, and competing on the swim team. A week or so before final exams, I stayed awake for a few nights to cram for the tests. Soon after, I found that I was missing meals, getting more irritable, and feeling an endless stream of uncontrollable thoughts and ideas. I talked a lot. My friends accused me of being self-centered. I was too busy to recognize it then, but my behavior had really changed.[11]

According to the *DSM-IV*, a manic episode is diagnosed if the over-elevated mood is accompanied by at least three other symptoms that last most of the day, almost every day, for at least one week, and it interferes with daily living. If the main mood is one of irritability, four of the other symptoms must be present to diagnose a manic episode.

People in the grip of a manic episode may become psychotic, that is, they may lose touch with reality. They may have hallucinations, in which they believe they see things that are not really there, or hear voices in their minds that tell them to do things they would never normally do. They may have delusional thoughts, which are irrational thoughts that cannot possibly be true. For example, they may believe that the Central Intelligence Agency is after them, or that their boss is an alien. Psychosis requires hospitalization to prevent the person from hurting himself or others. It can result in the destruction of the person's relationships with family and friends, loss of employment, and deliberate or accidental suicide.

Hypomania

Sometimes people with bipolar disorder experience a mood called hypomania, which is less extreme than mania. They may feel very good and have periods of unusual creativity and energy. They may be more outgoing and sociable than at other times. The symptoms of hypomania are not severe enough to interfere with daily living and do not include psychotic episodes. Because they feel so good, people in hypomania may deny that there is anything wrong. Without treatment, however, hypomania can progress into full mania or may switch to depression.

Degrees of Bipolar Disorder

Depending on the severity of the symptoms, bipolar disorder is generally classified into four types. Bipolar I is the most severe form. It includes episodes of extreme mania, either alone or combined with severe depression. There may be psychotic symptoms, and suicide is a significant risk with Bipolar I. Approximately 10 percent of Bipolar I sufferers succeed in ending their own lives.

Bipolar II is a somewhat less severe form. People with Bipolar II still may have episodes of major depression, but instead of full-blown mania, the person with Bipolar II is more likely to have episodes of hypomania. Their behavior is still erratic and unusual enough to be noticeable to others, and the risk of suicide is still high. They also tend to have more mood cycles in a year than those with Bipolar I.

A third and even milder form of bipolar disorder is called cyclothymia. Cyclothymia is similar to dysthymic depressive disorder in that, although the mood swings are less intense and the symptoms are milder, they may last for a much longer time. They must be present for at least two years in adults and at least one year in children and adolescents in order for cyclothymia to be diagnosed. Periods of normal mood do not last for more than two months at a time. In cyclothymia, the manic phase is similar to hypomania, and symptoms of the depressive phase are milder than in major depression. There is a 15 to 20 percent chance that a person with cyclothymia will later develop Bipolar I or Bipolar II.

A fourth form of bipolar disorder is called Bipolar NOS, or "not otherwise specified." This is diagnosed when a person has all the symptoms of a bipolar disorder, but does not meet all the clinical criteria that define one of the other disorders. For example, a teen may have classic signs of mania, but they last only three days and appear only once a month. Or a girl may have episodes of hypomania but never show depressive symptoms. Bipolar NOS is often diagnosed in children because the standards set forth in the *DSM-IV-TR* are based on adults, and children and teens do not always show the same kinds of symptoms as adults.

Cycling

The symptoms of bipolar disorder come and go in cycles of mood from high to low and back again. The term "cycling" refers to the length of time between episodes of mania and depression. Between cycles, the person may have a period of

People with rapid cycling experience extreme lows and highs, like having more energy or being more social, several times a year.

feeling calm and more "normal," neither manic nor depressed. Other people may never feel really normal, but may just feel less manic or less depressed between more intense episodes. About 20 percent of people with Bipolar I or Bipolar II have rapid cycling. This means that their high and low moods change at least four times in any twelve-month period. Others experience ultra-rapid cycling. These people may experience mood shifts several times each day. Rapid and ultra-rapid cycling can be very difficult to treat because of the frequent mood shifts.

Depression and bipolar disorders can be difficult to manage because of the wide range of symptoms involved and because the symptoms can be expressed very differently from person to person. Over the last thirty years, however, knowledge and understanding of these disorders has improved dramatically, leading to earlier and more accurate diagnosis and more effective treatment than ever before.

Diagnosis and Treatment

Mood disorders can evolve over time and may seem to "sneak up" on a person. The symptoms can start out rather mild and slowly worsen over time so that it may not even be noticeable to others that there is a problem until something sudden, such as a suicide attempt, happens. In addition, no two individuals experience symptoms in exactly the same way. It can be easy to miss the early warning signs that something is wrong. Thanks to increased awareness and knowledge about mood disorders, diagnosis and treatment of them has dramatically improved, and there is hope for a better life for the thousands of people who struggle with these kinds of illnesses.

Diagnosing Mood Disorders

The diagnosis of a mood disorder often begins when those involved in the affected person's life notice that he or she is behaving in ways that are not typical or usual for the person. When someone who has always been optimistic, sociable, and active suddenly seems sad or angry much of the time, friends and family may become concerned that something is wrong. Teens may wonder why their friend never wants to go out any more. Parents may wonder why their child is getting in trouble at school, why her grades are dropping, or why she shuts herself in her room and rarely interacts with the rest of the family. People at work may notice that their coworker frequently calls

Teens who develop a mood disorder may begin to have trouble in school, such a slipping grades.

in sick, that her moods change rapidly and drastically, or that her job performance is not what it should be.

If the unusual behavior does not stop on its own, concerned outsiders may bring the unusual behavior to the person's attention and encourage her to seek professional help. Sometimes the person herself may realize that there is a problem and go to a professional on her own. A child or teen in pain may ask a parent to get her the help she needs. In some cases, however, the problem may go unnoticed by anyone until the person does something drastic, such as self-mutilation or an attempt at suicide.

The Psychiatric Interview

The first step in diagnosing a mood disorder is the psychiatric interview. This is done by a mental health professional, either a psychiatrist or psychologist, in a private, comfortable setting in which the person can feel relaxed and at ease. It is critical that the person feel comfortable and safe with the interviewer so that she will be able to talk openly about what has been going on in her life. Eighteen-year-old Shannon was lucky to find a therapist she could connect with. "I see my therapist every week," she says. "And I actually look forward to it. She's really down to earth and approachable. We can talk about anything. She's always on my side. [W]hen I walk into her office each week, I know it's a place where I can relax. It's a place where no one judges me. And I can just be me."[12]

The psychiatric interview, however, is more than just a conversation. Much like a physical examination, it is a systematic mental health examination focusing on specific points of behavior for which the professional knows to look. The professional's goal is to learn as much as possible about the person's recent experiences, activities, and family history without being judgmental or critical. This first interview is not meant to offer advice or draw conclusions, but to help the professional begin to identify the problem, and to help the person become more aware of how the events in her past and present life have affected her.

There can be obstacles faced in a psychiatric interview, especially with younger people. One psychiatrist explains:

> With teenagers, there are hurdles in an interview that have to be overcome. Kids can be angry with adults, or even just reluctant to talk on the general principle that adults are as a group untrustworthy. Often I can see a youngster sizing me up when he first meets me, trying to determine whether I am a potential ally or just another adult to be wary of. On the other hand, there can be a sense of relief when a kid sees that you can be a possible advocate, and with that realization the reluctance to discuss the problems can begin to disappear.[13]

In cases where the person is reluctant or unwilling to talk with the doctor, the professional may also want to interview family members or teachers. When the patient is a young child, play interviews may be done, in which the child is encouraged to act out her feelings using toys, role-playing, or art.

Ruling Out Physical Causes

When the initial interview indicates that a person may be suffering from a mood disorder, other diseases that might cause the symptoms must be ruled out before treatment can begin. The mental health professional may ask questions about the person's medical history and any illness for which she has been treated. Children may then be referred to their pediatrician, and teens and adults may be sent to their internist or family doctor for a thorough physical checkup to make sure there is not a physical illness that could be causing the psychiatric symptoms.

After the initial interview and the physical examination, the doctor may consult the *DSM-IV* to see how the patient's symptoms and their intensity and duration compare to the descriptions in the manual. It is not enough, however, to follow the guidelines in the *DSM-IV*, particularly when it comes to chil-

It is important for doctors to rule out a physical reason which may be causing symptoms similar to those caused by mood disorders before beginning treatment.

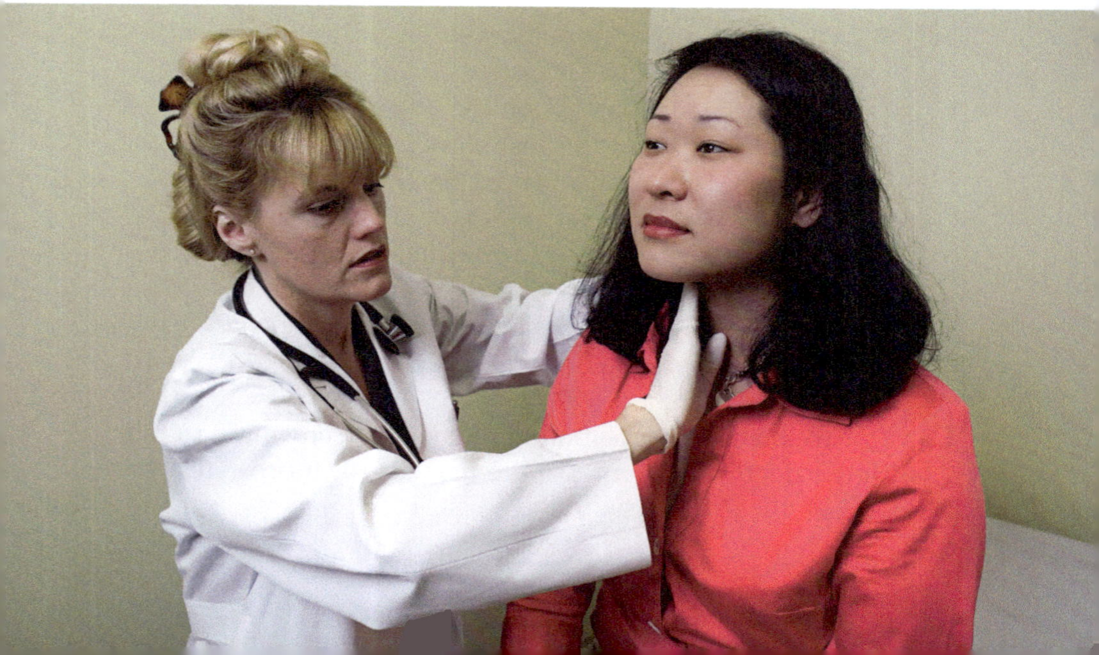

dren and teens. Physical and emotional signs—oversleeping, weight loss or gain, the occasional headache or stomachache, moodiness and irritability—are not necessarily signs of depression or bipolar disorder. They are often just a normal part of being an adolescent. Other tools are sometimes necessary. One of these is the mental health inventory.

The Mental Health Professional

The management of a mood disorder is best done by a person specially trained in this kind of work. There are several different kinds of mental health professionals available who help people learn to cope with and solve their problems. The choice of a professional depends on the specific needs of the individual and his personal feelings about psychological and chemical treatments. The most important thing is that the person chooses someone with whom he can be comfortable enough to be open and honest.

Most mental health treatment is managed by either a psychiatrist or a psychologist. Psychiatrists and psychologists are both highly trained and licensed mental health professionals. Both can diagnose psychiatric illnesses, discuss treatment options, and develop an individualized plan for treatment. A psychiatrist is a physician with a medical degree, along with at least six additional years of training in psychiatry. As a physician, he or she can prescribe medications such as antidepressants and mood stabilizers. A psychologist is someone who has an average of seven years of specialized mental health training after college before receiving a doctorate degree, followed by at least one year of supervised training before she can practice on her own. Psychologists do not prescribe medications, but they may recommend a prescription that the patient can receive from his regular doctor. Psychologists focus more on talk therapy to bring about healthy changes in a person's outlook and responses to life stresses so that he can eventually learn to manage his stresses on his own.

Mental Health Inventories

Mental health inventories are like questionnaires that can be completed by either the doctor or the patient. They are well-designed and require extensive training on the part of the professional in order to use and interpret them properly. They help with diagnosis by providing a written record (or inventory) of the patient's feelings, physical symptoms, and daily experiences. Two inventories used widely by health professionals for diagnosing depression are the Hamilton Depression Scale and the Montgomery and Asberg Depression Rating Scale. These scales provide a list of symptoms that the doctor rates from 0 to 4 (Hamilton) or 0 to 7 (Montgomery and Asberg), depending on the intensity of the symptom. The scales are also useful for tracking the progress of the patient as she goes through treatment. Scales for helping to diagnose bipolar disorder include the Bipolar Spectrum Diagnostic Scale, the Young Mania Rating Scale, and the Mood Disorders Questionnaire.

Teens can rate themselves using one of several inventories, such as the Beck Depression Inventory, the Carroll Rating Scale, the Zung Self-Rating Depression Scale, and the Inventory for Depressive Symptomatology. Most of these scales list statements, such as "I feel the world would be better off without me," or "I have trouble sleeping through the night." Teens evaluate each statement as to how they apply to their own experiences. There are scales especially designed for children, and parents may be asked to complete parent versions of these scales. There are also scales specifically for the elderly, and for diagnosing postpartum depression and seasonal affective disorder.

Many people live with a mood disorder for years before it is accurately diagnosed. Diagnosis of mood disorders can be difficult and complicated. To do it right requires years of training and experience, along with cooperation from the individual and his family. Once the diagnosis is correctly made, however, effective treatment can begin.

Talk Therapies

Talk therapies are the most common treatment method for mood disorders. Talk therapies may be used alone or in combination with medication. The patient meets with the professional, either alone or in a group, on a regular schedule. Together, they identify the specific problems the patient is having and come up with healthier ways of dealing with those concerns. There

A common form of treatment for mood disorders is known as talk therapy. This is where a patient meets with a professional to discuss problems and solutions dealing with the person's disorder.

are several different types of talk therapy, including individual psychotherapy, group therapy, and family therapy. The choice of therapy depends on the individual situation for each patient.

Individual psychotherapy allows for one-on-one interaction between the patient and his therapist. There are many different approaches to and theories about psychotherapy, with a lot of overlapping of concepts, and a therapist may choose to use a combination of approaches to treat the patient. Research suggests that the most effective approach is cognitive-behavioral therapy. Cognitive behavior therapy (CBT) is based on the idea that it is a person's thoughts that affect how he behaves and how he views his world, rather than outside events, situations, or other people. It is focused on changing how a person thinks about these things so that he can deal with them in a healthier way, even if the situations themselves do not change. The person learns that there are alternative ways to view any situation, and that things may not always be as bad as he thinks. This allows the person to cope better with whatever might come up in the future. Unlike traditional psychotherapy, which can last for years, CBT has been shown to achieve effective results in as little as a few months, after which the formal therapy ends and the patient sees the therapist only if he needs extra support. CBT is particularly effective for treating depression and is a valuable therapy, in combination with medication, for bipolar disorder.

Group therapy involves a professional meeting with a small group of people who all struggle with similar problems. Group therapy has several advantages. Groups provide support for the members and a chance to see that they are not alone in their struggle. They can benefit from seeing how others are coping with their issues and can learn from one another. Members who may be reluctant to talk can choose to participate only when they feel comfortable enough to speak up. Eighteen-year-old Heather had to be hospitalized because of her bipolar disorder. "The doctors there helped me a lot," she says, "but it was the other kids who were the greatest comfort. We all understood each other. For the first time, I didn't feel like a freak."[14]

Expressed Emotion

One concept sometimes used in family therapy is expressed emotion (EE). Expressed emotion is a term that describes the quality of a person's relationship with his family. It is considered by many therapists to be an indicator of how likely a patient is to have a relapse after successful treatment. The theory is that the higher the level of expressed emotion, measured using a family interview technique, the more likely the patient is to have a relapse of his illness.

EE examines three attitudes of family members: hostility, criticalness, and emotional over-involvement. Hostility means that the family has a negative or angry attitude toward the patient. They may blame him and his illness for the problems in the family and accuse of him of being selfish because he does not "choose" to get better. Criticalness involves statements of dislike, annoyance, or resentment of the patient because of his disorder. Emotional over-involvement means that the family may actually blame themselves for the patient's troubles and feel responsible for it. They become too involved and overbearing in the patient's life, which can cause even more stress for the patient. EE is controversial because research studies have not reached consistent results, and professionals disagree about its value in family therapy

Family Therapy

Sometimes a therapist may want to spend time with both the patient and his family. This allows the therapist to learn more about what kinds of problems may be occurring within the family, how the family members relate to one another, and what kind of effects these things may be having on the patient. Family therapy also helps the family members understand and cope with the disorder and teaches them how to communicate in healthier ways, solve problems, and help and support each other. The mother of a teenage boy with depression says, "Therapy has helped us to be more in tune with Kevin's needs. My husband and I have learned to put less pressure on Kevin at school. We listen to him now and try to see things from his perspective rather than only from our perspective as parents. We're trying not to play down the things that bother him. They are important to him at this age. We are learning to understand and respect that."[15]

Medications for Mood Disorders

When depression is very severe or if the patient is struggling with bipolar disorder, talk therapies may not be enough, and medications are added to the treatment plan. Medications work by balancing the levels of neurotransmitters in the brain, allowing for clearer and more realistic thinking and feeling to take place. This helps the patient to be more responsive to talk therapies and to participate in them more actively. Medications used for treating mood disorders include antidepressants and mood stabilizers.

Antidepressants

Antidepressant medications are used to treat all forms of depression. They are not the same as stimulants, or "uppers," in that they have no effect on people who are not depressed, and they are not addictive. They help restore the proper levels of neurotransmitters in the brain to where they were before the depression began. They do this in several different ways. Some act by slowing the chemical breakdown of neurotransmitters. Others prevent the reuptake, or reabsorption, of neurotransmitters by the neuron that released it. Still others increase the amount of neurotransmitters released at the ends of the neurons. Antidepressants are divided into three main categories: monoamine oxidase inhibitors (MAOIs), tricyclic antidepressants, and selective serotonin reuptake inhibitors (SSRIs).

MAOIs were the first antidepressants. They include such drugs as phenelzine (Nardil), isocarboxazid (Marplan), and tranylcypromine (Parnate). MAOIs block the breakdown of

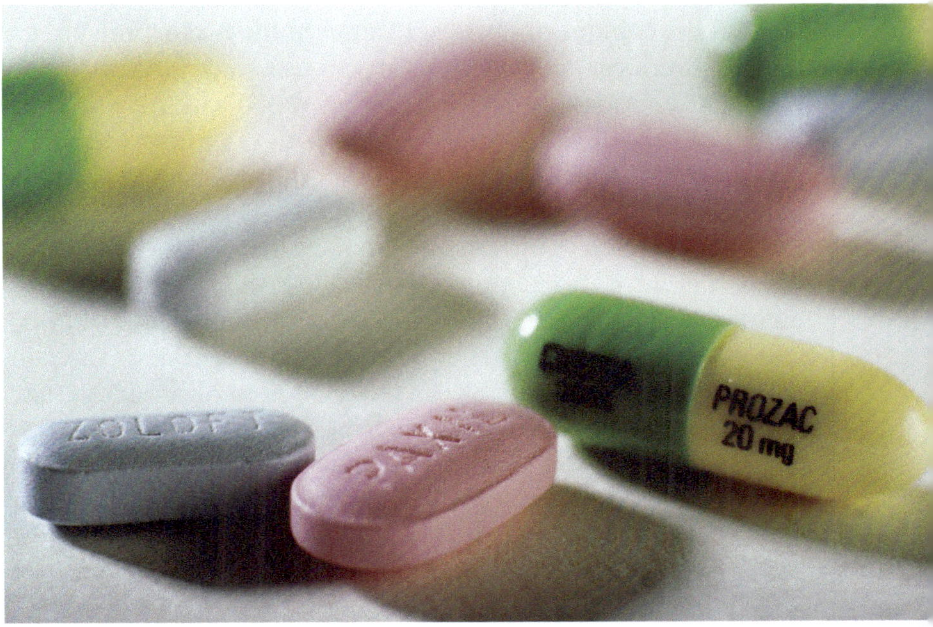

The three most commonly prescribed SSRI antidepressants are Zoloft, Paxil, and Prozac.

norepinephrine and serotonin in the brain by an enzyme called monoamine oxidase. This helps restore their levels to normal. The main drawback to these drugs is that they cannot be taken in combination with certain foods that contain high amounts of the amino acid tyramine, such as hot dogs and other processed meats, soy products, aged cheese, chocolate, wine, and beer. They also cannot be taken with some medications including cough medicines, diet pills, and allergy medications. Combining MAOIs with these foods and medicines can cause a very serious reaction that includes high blood pressure, chest pain, headache, and vomiting. Because of these side effects, MAOIs are rarely prescribed in the United States, especially for children and teens, and then only as a last resort if other medications failed to work.

Tricyclics are among the earliest antidepressants to be developed. They include such medications as imipramine (Tofranil) and desipramine (Norpramin) and work by raising the level of norepinephrine and serotonin in the brain. Side effects include dizziness, weight gain, dry mouth, and constipation. A potentially serious side effect is interference with the electrical activity of the heart. Because of this, an overdose of a tricyclic medication can be lethal, and the therapist must consider whether or not his patient is suicidal before prescribing them.

SSRIs were first introduced in 1988 and by the mid-2000s were the most frequently prescribed antidepressants. They include drugs such as fluoxetine (Prozac), sertraline (Zoloft), and paroxetine (Paxil). They prevent the reuptake of the neurotransmitter serotonin. SSRIs have fewer serious side effects than tricyclics and cause less harm if taken in overdose. Prozac has also been shown to help young people with anxiety disorders and obsessive-compulsive disorder (OCD). The main side effects of SSRIs are occasional headaches or nausea, but some patients have reported feeling overstimulated at times, and Prozac has actually been known to cause manic symptoms in some people.

In the early to mid-2000s some SSRIs were linked with increased incidences of worsening depression and suicide, especially in younger patients. Research as of 2007 has not provided a definite answer as to how significant the risk is. In 2004 the Federal Drug Administration ordered the makers of SSRI drugs to include warnings about this risk on the drug labels. Most therapists, however, consider it safer to prescribe these medications and monitor their patients closely rather than have them take no medication for their depression.

Drugs for Bipolar Disorder

Unlike depression, which can sometimes be treated with talk therapies alone, treatment for bipolar disorders must include medications called mood stabilizers. Mood stabilizers help to even out, or stabilize, the radical mood swings of bipolar disorder and decrease their frequency. Like antidepressants, they work by normalizing levels of neurotransmitters in the brain. Also like antidepressants, mood stabilizers can take several weeks to begin working so doctors often prescribe other drugs, such as sleep aids or mild sedatives, to help with the symptoms until the mood stabilizer takes effect. Antidepressants are sometimes prescribed along with mood stabilizers. Antidepressants are not generally used alone in bipolar disorder, however, because they run the risk of switching the patient into mania or hypomania, or of starting rapid cycling.

The most common medication for treating bipolar disorder is lithium. Lithium is a naturally occurring element that was first found to control mania in 1949. It is especially effective for people who experience pure mania, without depression. It is not as effective for those with rapid-cycling bipolar disorder. Lithium has several side effects. It can cause thirst, water retention, nausea, diarrhea, weight gain, and hand tremors. It has been known to cause birth defects if taken during pregnancy. More serious side effects include kidney disease, hypothyroidism, and skin problems. For these reasons, doctors try to use only the smallest dose of lithium that is still effective to control the patient's symptoms.

Although first developed as a treatment for seizures, Tegretol is now often used to treat patients with bipolar disorder.

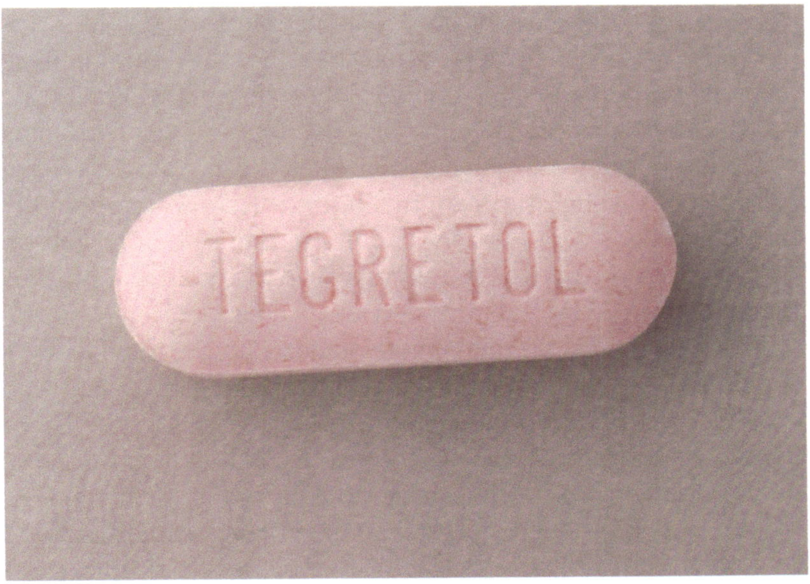

Since the 1990s, several newer drugs have been developed for treating bipolar disorders. Valproate (Depakote) was first used as a treatment for seizures. It is much more effective in treating mania than depression, so it is often prescribed for milder forms of bipolar such as cyclothymia and Bipolar II. It is less toxic than lithium and takes effect faster. It also helps with rapid-cycling episodes. A patient using Valproate must be closely monitored, however, because it can cause liver problems and fevers. Carbamazepine (Tegretol) also began as a treatment for seizures. It has helped some patients for whom other drugs have been ineffective. Its major side effect is a rare but potentially fatal skin reaction called Stevens-Johnson Syndrome, which starts with flu-like symptoms and progresses to a blistering skin rash and possible organ damage. Other newer drugs for bipolar include gabapentin, topiramate, and lamotrigine. These drugs treat both depression and mania and are not toxic to the body.

Electroconvulsive Therapy

The development of more effective drugs for mood disorders has revolutionized the treatment of these disorders over the last fifteen to twenty years, but for some people with severe forms of bipolar disorder or depression, talk therapies and medications may not be effective enough. In such cases another alternative is electroconvulsive therapy (ECT). ECT involves using electrodes attached to the patient's skull to send a mild electrical current through the patient's brain for about one minute. How it works is not entirely understood, but doctors believe that the current changes the chemistry in the brain and relieves the symptoms of both depression and mania.

Far from the frightening image depicted in the movies, ECT is painless, safe, and highly effective, with few unpleasant side effects. The procedure is done in the hospital with the patient under general anesthesia so that he feels nothing. After the patient wakes up, he may have sore muscles, headache, or some temporary confusion or memory loss. Usually, several treatments are necessary to achieve the desired results, after which the patient takes medications to keep his symptoms under control.

ECT is especially effective for patients who are extremely depressed or suicidal, or in a state of severe mania. It is recommended for those who are resistant to medications or for women with bipolar who are pregnant. It is used much more often for adults than for teens or children. In the late 1980's, doctors discovered that ECT is effective even if only one side of the brain is stimulated. The patient wakes up faster and has fewer side effects. In some countries, such as Great Britain, ECT is actually used as a first-line treatment, before medications.

Light Therapy for SAD

Another treatment method, specifically for Seasonal Affective Disorder (SAD), is light therapy, also called phototherapy. SAD occurs most frequently during the winter months, when the hours of daylight are less. One of the most effective treatments for SAD involves spending about half an hour each day sitting in front of a light box specially designed for people with SAD.

A patient using light therapy to treat his Seasonal Affective Disorder. For many patients, light therapy is so effective that medication is not needed to treat the disorder.

The light box uses fluorescent bulbs that emit a high intensity light similar to outdoor light. It is not the same kind of light made by regular household lamps. Exposure to the light produced by these fluorescent bulbs changes the chemistry in the brain and eases the symptoms of SAD by helping to lift mood, improve concentration, and increase energy.

There are several advantages to light therapy. For many people with SAD, light therapy is effective enough that antidepressants are not necessary. No prescription is needed to buy a light box. The treatment can be done when convenient for the patient and can be done in the patient's own home while reading, watching television, or talking on the phone. There are, however, some drawbacks. It may not be effective for everyone, and talk therapy or medication may still be necessary. Light therapy has been known to trigger manic episodes in people who are bipolar. In addition, light therapy may have side effects such as eyestrain, headache, nausea, irritability, and insomnia. Patients should discuss it with their doctor before trying it.

Mood disorders are lifelong conditions with which many people struggle on a daily basis. Although they are, as yet, not curable, they are manageable with proper diagnosis and appropriate treatment. Living with a mood disorder need not be the difficult situation it was in the past.

Living with Mood Disorders

People with depression or bipolar disorders ride a roller coaster of emotions that significantly impact their daily lives. Relationships within the family can be strained or sometimes even damaged beyond repair. Children and teens struggle to get along with parents and friends and to do well in school. When a mood disorder interferes with work, it may be difficult to hold down a job. Mood disorders, as with other mental illnesses, still carry with them a social stigma, which can make it difficult for the person to admit he has a problem and to seek help for it. All these things isolate the person with a mood disorder from sources of support and help. Fortunately, methods of diagnosis and treatment have dramatically improved, and sources of help and support abound for those who seek it.

The Stigma of Mental Illness

One of the greatest barriers to getting help for a mood disorder is the stigma, or shame, associated with having a mental illness. Often, people with symptoms of depression or mania fear that they are crazy, weak, or a failure at life. They may be ashamed to tell anyone about their symptoms and may be afraid to seek help. "I was very good at putting on a façade [outward show] for people," says Julie, who suffered with depression for more than twenty years. "There's a stigma. People look at you differently, like [you're] a crazy person. I didn't want the stigma

People with mood disorders may not be able to keep a job because their symptoms prevent them from doing their work effectively.

placed on me. People don't understand. It's a disease, just like cancer."[16]

Mental illnesses such as mood disorders are different from other illnesses, however, in that they are manifested mostly in behavior patterns rather than in physical symptoms, like most illnesses or injury. As a consequence, many people think that a person showing signs of depression or mania is feeling sorry for himself or is trying to get attention. Others may be quick to criticize or judge those with a mood disorder. They think the person ought to be able to control his own behavior. "Some people don't look at depression as an illness," says eighteen-year-old Shannon. "They think you are just being moody or lazy. They think it's a weakness and you should be able to pull yourself out of it."[17] These disorders, however, are true illnesses, and, without treatment, a person with a mood disorder cannot control his feelings or behavior any more than he could control cancer or a broken ankle.

Because of the stigma still attached to mental illness, parents may resist the idea that their child or teen could have an emotional disorder, even when the child tells them something is wrong and asks for help. This can cause a long delay in obtaining a diagnosis and treatment "If a child had a headache for two weeks," says one psychiatrist, "his parents wouldn't expect him to snap out of it. They'd send him to a doctor. But there is still a feeling that depression isn't serious and it will go away by itself."[18]

As with any other illness, the person with a mood disorder needs understanding and support. One of the most important keys to understanding mood disorders and overcoming the stigma attached to them is education for the patient and for all those involved in his life.

Learning about Mood Disorders

Finding out as much information as possible about mood disorders helps the patient and those around him understand his illness and manage the symptoms. Knowledge helps the patient find the help and support he needs. Education can be found by attending therapy sessions, reading books, watching videos, contacting mental health organizations, and joining support groups.

Fifty-three-year-old Wendy started her own bipolar support group after being hospitalized for a severe depressive episode.

One of the most important ways to treat mood disorders is to educate not only patients, but family members, by using methods such as support groups.

Besides providing an opportunity for bipolar patients to support one another, the group also provides education. "One of the most important things we can do with friends and family members is to educate them," says Wendy. "What you don't know, you're afraid of. It's like any prejudice." Adds her husband, Ralf, "The biggest problem is not knowing about it. The more they know, the easier it is to cope with it. I talk to Wendy a lot because I want to know about it. It's a constant learning process."[19]

Family Matters

A very important source of support for the person with a mood disorder is his own family. There is well-established evidence that parents who have suffered with depression are more likely than other parents to have children with the tendency to develop the same disorder. It can be very upsetting to a child or teen to think that he has inherited his problem from his parent, and he may be tempted to blame the parent for his troubles and resent him or her for it. Parents, however, cannot, by their behavior, cause their children to become depressed. Not all children of depressed parents develop depression, and not all children who are depressed have parents with the same disorder.

Although family members do not cause depression, it is clear that difficult family situations can be associated with depression. Divorce, high levels of stress in the mother, and poor relationships with a father can lead to depression in susceptible teens. Seventeen-year-old Jeff recalls:

> I was in tenth grade when my parents split up. That's when I really started to get depressed. After my dad left, my schoolwork started getting worse. I was sleeping a lot, and I was always in a bad mood. Nothing made me happy, even baseball, which I love… Nothing seemed fun; nothing seemed interesting, no matter what I did. I knew something was wrong because I'm not a gloomy kid. But when my parents split up, everything got really bad.[20]

Help for Families

Families have a very important part in the effective treatment of mood disorders. For treatment to succeed, the family must be united, supportive, patient, and uncritical in their approach to the person with the disorder. Families can help by having a hopeful, optimistic outlook that the person can get better. They should not blame the person for his illness or for the problems within the family; as hard as these disorders are on the family, they are harder for the person affected by them. At the same time, the person should not be allowed to use his illness as an excuse for not participating in his own treatment. Family members can also help the person by making sure he takes his medication as prescribed and keeps his therapy appointments.

Family members may need help themselves in order to understand and cope with the challenges of a mood disorder. It can be very upsetting for family members to see their loved one so depressed that he cannot get out of bed. They may want

Parents whose children have been diagnosed with a mood disorder often feel guilty that they are somehow responsible for causing their child's illness.

to help the person, but feel helpless and unable to do anything. Parents may struggle with guilt, fearful that they are somehow responsible for their child's illness either genetically or by how they raised their child. One mother of a depressed teen recalls:

> Once I found out that Jordynn was depressed, I realized that my mother had suffered from depression off and on through the years…, and there were times my mother's aunt would also sit for long periods without any activity. Thinking back on it, I'm sure they were depressed. But no one talked about it. Now that Jordynn has been diagnosed with depression, I feel somewhat responsible. She must have inherited the tendency from my side of the family.[21]

Brothers and sisters of a depressed child or teen also struggle. They may not be old enough or mature enough to be able to understand what is happening to their sibling. They may feel guilty that they may have done something to make their sibling feel so bad. Some may become angry and resentful because of the extra attention their sibling receives. Brothers and sisters of bipolar children and teens may feel embarrassed about their sibling's manic behavior or afraid of their sudden outbursts of anger.

When a parent is depressed, family relationships can become strained and confused. Some depressed parents become irritable and impatient with their children. They may become withdrawn and neglectful and fail to set the limits and guidelines that children need. In single-family homes in which the only parent is depressed, the depressed parent may be unable to fulfill the roles and responsibilities of raising children, and the child or teen may take on some of the parental role. This adds a great deal of stress to an already stressful time in a young person's life. Some children may react with anger or resentment toward the depressed parent. Communication breaks down, and arguments are frequent.

Bipolar disorder can be especially confusing and upsetting to the family because they cannot predict how the person will behave from one moment to the next. They may also have to deal with the consequences of serious or even illegal misbehavior committed while the person is manic. Family therapy with a well-trained and experienced family therapist can go a long way toward helping family members deal with all of these issues.

Pet Therapy

Animals such as cats and dogs have long been used by nursing homes and hospitals to help residents overcome depressed feelings. The presence of a well-trained and well-behaved animal can have a soothing effect on a person, especially for children, and especially if the person can hold or pet the animal during therapy sessions.

Outside the therapist's office, specially trained pets, certified as Emotional Support Animals, can live with the patient and go with him wherever he goes. Certified pets can go with their people on busses and planes, and many hotels allow therapy animals to stay in the hotel room with the person.

Pets can help a person get through his days with less anxiety. Caring for an animal helps distract the person from stresses and gives them a sense of purpose and responsibility. As most pet owners already know, pets, especially dogs, have a natural desire to please people, and the love and devotion that they provide comes without conditions or judgments. The companionship and unconditional love provided by another living creature can be therapeutic for a person living with depression.

Pets, such as dogs, are being used in nursing homes, hospitals, and even in patients' own homes to help cope with depression.

Help From Friends

A good friend can be a major source of support for a depressed child or teen, sometimes even more than his parents. Unfortunately, mood disorders can have a negative effect on his ability to make and keep friends. Most kids do not like to be around someone who is withdrawn and sad all the time, and does not want to participate in activities. If the child or teen is irritable, argumentative, or quick to anger, other children will likely want to avoid him. Depressed teens may struggle with dating or keeping a boyfriend or girlfriend. Being rejected and shunned by classmates can make the child feel even more worthless, which can worsen his depression.

Friends can help a depressed peer by encouraging him, by inviting him to participate in activities, and just by being there for him to listen if he wants to talk. It is not enough, however, to just tell him to cheer up and smile. "I hate when people tell me that I should get over this and be happy," says fifteen-year-old Kevin. "I want to say, 'Don't you think I've tried that?'"[22] Many times, the problems are beyond the ability of another child to solve. A friend can also help by talking to a responsible adult such as a trusted teacher, school nurse, or guidance counselor, especially if the depressed friend has talked about hurting himself in any way.

Help at School

Children with depression often struggle in school. Depression can cause a child to experience difficulty concentrating or remembering things. Missing school days because of fatigue, sleeplessness, stomachaches, or headaches makes keeping up at school more challenging. Feelings of worthlessness, hopelessness, or futility make it difficult for the child to care about getting good grades. Frustration because of such problems at school can cause a child to react with misbehavior or hostility toward others. His behavior may make him a target for bullying and teasing. As a result, self-esteem falls, creating a cycle of failure, embarrassment, frustration, and anger. Many children with mood disorders may skip school to avoid further failure.

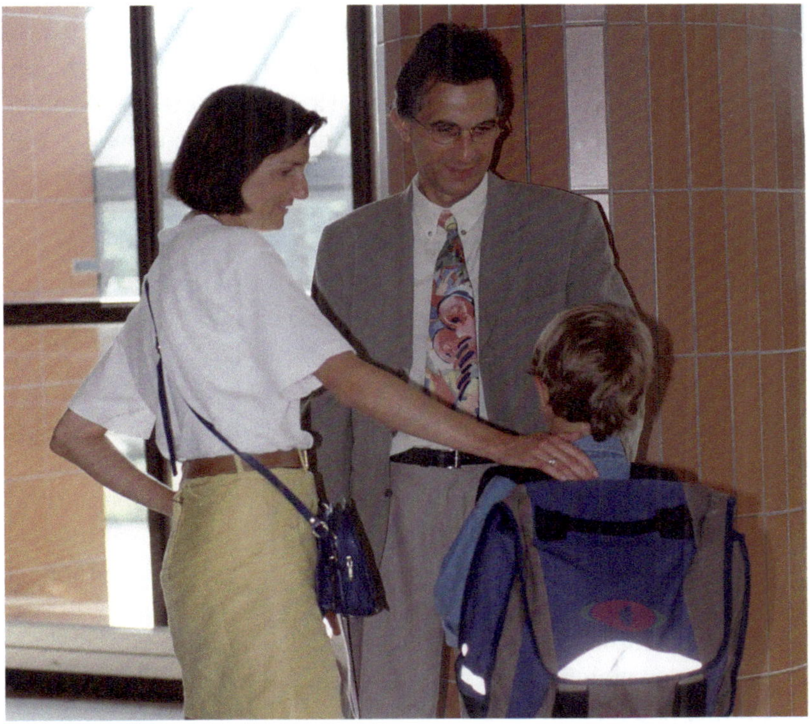

Teachers working closely with parents and students who suffer from mood disorders can help these students cope with their illness at school.

Some drop out. Teachers can help by keeping communication open with the student and his parents, creating a caring, supportive, and nurturing environment in the classroom, and providing frequent praise and encouragement for the struggling student.

Help at Work

After school is over, the person with depression or bipolar disorder enters the adult world. This includes getting and keeping a job. The struggle to succeed at work can be just as stressful for the adult as the struggle to succeed in school was for the student. People with mood disorders who have jobs may be afraid to tell their employer about their illness, fearful that they will be fired or passed over for promotions. For those with depression, just getting up and getting to work can at times seem impossible. Julie spent much of the 1990s in her bedroom with the blinds drawn, unable to work. "I'd get up in the morning," she says. "I'd get my kids off to school. I'd go back to bed until my kids came home from school. I cried all the time. I couldn't do anything."[23]

Bipolar disorders have a different set of challenges that can affect getting and keeping a job. "People with bipolar disorders often feel they can do things no one else can do," says psychology professor David J. Miklowitz.

> They may sleep less than usual—or not at all—and may have great energy, talk faster and express unrealistic ideas. Some may be easily distracted and act impulsively by spending money unwisely or driving recklessly. On the down side, those with bipolar disorder may feel extremely sad, irritable or anxious. They may lose interest in people or activities, sleep too much or be unable to sleep. Energy levels may be low. Some may feel bad or guilty, and a few talk about committing suicide—or even act on these thoughts.[24]

All these things can have an impact on a person's ability to do his job.

There is help available for people struggling with mood disorders who want to return to the workforce. The great majority of adults living with a mood disorder want to hold jobs. "Of the people we see here, no matter how low their functioning—three-quarters of them, their goal is to someday work," says Mala Spivack, clinical director of the North Jersey Friendship House, a New Jersey organization devoted to helping the psychologically disabled find work. "Clearly, across the board, it's an important value for people...."[25] Sabina, a woman with depression so severe she had to be hospitalized, found a way to rebuild her life, including employment.

> I began by registering in a Work Adjustment Employment Support program run by a local psychiatric hospital. I was

placed in a volunteer work placement at the hospital. The volunteer job gave me a structure to my day. [It] gave me a reason to get out of bed every morning and get dressed. It also gave me some recent work experience to put on my resume." Eventually, she found a full time job in her field. "It had taken three years since my release from the hospital to find a meaningful career. If I could do it, others can, too.[26]

Compliance with Treatment

One of the most important keys to success at home, at school, and at work is compliance with treatment. This means following closely the plan set up for the patient by the doctor, and staying with it every day. Studies show that 80 percent of people who seek treatment for depression are successfully treated. In order for treatment to work, however, the person must stick with the treatment plan and take an active part in his own therapy.

Compliance can be difficult, especially for those with bipolar disorders. Taking prescribed medication exactly as the doctor orders is necessary for successful treatment of bipolar disorder, but after several weeks of talk therapy and medication, patients usually begin to feel better and may begin to doubt their need for more treatment. Bipolar patients may miss the good feeling experience when in a state of hypomania and may feel that the medication is stifling the energy and creativity they feel in that state. They may decide that the benefits of their medications are not worth suffering the side effects. If a person with bipolar stops taking his medication, his symptoms will eventually return, and they may be worse than before. If he returns to the medication, it may not work as well. Compliance with treatment is a critical part of successful recovery.

Managing the Symptoms of Mood Disorders

Sometimes patients do not maintain their treatment because it can be expensive, and therapy can be time-consuming. In addition, because the symptoms of mood disorders vary from

Taking medications as prescribed is just one of the ways that patients can successfully treat mood disorders.

person to person, not all therapies work for all patients. As a result, patients often seek other ways to manage their symptoms, such as vitamin and herbal dietary supplements, hypnosis, exercise, and yoga.

Dietary Supplements

Vitamin and mineral deficiencies can cause symptoms of depression. Correcting these deficiencies, when present, often relieves depression. Even if there is no deficiency, sometimes vitamin supplements can improve symptoms in depressed patients. The B vitamins—B6, B12, and folic acid—can normalize levels of neurotransmitters in the brain, and B12 has been shown to alleviate postpartum depression in some women. Vitamin C improves serotonin levels, and magnesium can relieve depressive symptoms as well as symptoms of premenstrual syndrome (PMS).

St. John's Wort

St. John's wort is a natural herb that contains a chemical called hyperacin, which seems to have an effect similar to MAOIs in increasing serotonin levels, though without the side effects. St. John's wort can be taken as a pill or the whole plant can be used to make a tea. Its major drawback is that it can interfere with the action of other drugs, most importantly birth control pills, blood-thinning medications, and medications used to treat HIV, the virus that causes AIDS. Although research has shown that St. John's wort works better than placebos (pills used in research that do not contain any actual medication), and as well as or better than the tricyclic drug imipramine, more research is needed. Health care professionals recommend that people consult their doctor before taking it.

Hypnosis

Hypnosis is a state of relaxation and focused concentration in which a person becomes less aware of his surroundings and more aware of his own thoughts and feelings. It does not cure disease, but is used to help control symptoms of physical and

Ten Healthy Ways to Reduce Stress

1. **Take a walk.** Walking and other exercise leads to the release of endorphins. Even at a slow pace, most people notice an improvement in mood after just a few minutes of exercise.
2. **Meditate.** Relax in a comfortable position in a quiet place with no distractions and concentrate on a soft sound or on slow, deep breathing for five to twenty minutes. Meditation relaxes both the mind and the body. Yoga is a form of meditation.
3. **Listen to music.** Soothing, quiet music can be a very effective way to release stress.
4. **Decrease burdens** by not taking on any more tasks or responsibilities than what is absolutely necessary. Divide large tasks into smaller, more manageable steps, and take them one at a time.
5. **Laugh.** Watch a funny TV show, read a book of jokes, or go to a funny movie with friends. Laughter has been shown to reduce stress hormones such as cortisol and to increase endorphins.
6. **Develop a hobby.** Having a creative outlet such as painting or writing increases pleasure in life and helps release stress.
7. **Eat a healthy, balanced diet**. Eating right controls weight, increases energy and strength, and helps one feel better physically, which improves mood.
8. **Avoid self-medication** with chemicals such as alcohol, tobacco, and drugs. They can increase irritability and interfere with prescribed medications.
9. **Get enough sleep**, but do not oversleep. Eight to ten hours is about average.
10. **Talk to someone**. Confiding feelings to a trusted friend or family member goes a long way toward releasing stress and finding emotional support.

mental illness, to relieve pain, and to help people lose weight and stop smoking. It has been recognized as a valid therapy for certain conditions since 1958.

Hypnosis can be done by a licensed hypnotherapist, or the therapist can teach the person how to do self-hypnosis. Contrary to popular myths, the person does not fall asleep. The therapist does not "control" the hypnotized person and cannot make the person do things he would not ordinarily do. Hypnosis simply creates a state in which the mind becomes very relaxed, less distracted by outside stimuli and unhealthy thoughts, and more open to suggestions from the therapist that seem like reality. It has been compared to daydreaming, in which the person is fully conscious, but unaware of his surroundings.

It is not clear exactly how hypnosis works to change mood, but it is thought that it causes the brain to release chemicals that affect the way a person perceives symptoms. Another theory is that hypnosis relaxes the conscious mind, with all its thoughts, inhibitions, and distractions, and allows access to the subconscious mind, where a person is not even aware of decisions that are made. In this way, the person can learn to respond to his emotions in a healthier, more constructive way, and avoid the symptoms of depression.

Exercise

Exercise is one of the easiest and least costly methods for managing symptoms of depression. Aerobic exercise stimulates the release of endorphins in the brain. This accounts for the feeling of well-being that many people get after running, the so-called "runner's high." Fourteen-year-old Katherine describes the feeling she gets from running with her track team: "Running isn't just a sport," she says. "It's also like therapy. Those summer mornings, I felt peaceful and calm. My mind was at ease. I could think about my day. Or I could think about nothing at all."[27] Exercise also gets the body in shape and boosts self-esteem. It provides an opportunity for social contact with other people, and it helps to relieve day-to-day stress. Research done in 2000 at Duke University showed that exercise significantly reduces the chances that a person who has been treated for depression will have a relapse.

Yoga

One form of nonaerobic exercise that has been shown to be helpful is yoga. It works in a way similar to hypnosis in that it relaxes the body and mind and helps the person eliminate unhealthy patterns of thinking. Research at the Boston University School of Medicine in 2007 showed that practicing yoga actually increases levels of a brain neurotransmitter called gamma-aminobutyric acid (GABA).

Not all professionals agree on the effectiveness of yoga, but many agree that it can be helpful when combined with more traditional therapies such as cognitive behavioral therapy (CBT) and medication. One study done at the University of Toronto found that patients who used yoga along with CBT

Yoga is a nontraditional treatment that some professionals are using to treat mood disorders.

were less likely to have a relapse into depression than those who used CBT alone. “This means that people can learn about their emotions not just by writing down their thoughts, which is what cognitive therapy is all about,” says the director of the study, “but also by paying attention to the way their emotions are expressed in their bodies. Both approaches allow people to observe their experiences without judgment, an important first step in stepping out of depression.”[28]

CHAPTER FIVE

On the Horizon

Knowledge and understanding of mood disorders has come far in the last several decades. More accurate diagnosis, more effective treatment methods, and better education for patients, families, and the general public have helped to decrease the stigma and mystery surrounding these disorders and have helped to make living with a mood disorder much more manageable.

Research is the key toward achieving these goals. It allows scientists and health care professionals to learn and understand more about mood disorders. Through research, scientists and doctors have learned that mood disorders are, in fact, disorders of the brain. As of October 2007, more than 22,000 studies related to bipolar disorders and over 98,000 studies on depression have been published in medical journals around the world. Research related to mood disorders takes place in several areas and involves the participation of professionals in many different scientific and technological fields. Most research studies are done in the fields of neuroscience, genetic studies, and clinical studies.

Neuroscience is the study of the human brain's chemical, physical, and electrical structure. Neuroscientific studies shed light on how treatment methods work in the brain and on the biological causes of mood disorders that take place there.

An estimated one third to one half of all human genetic activity is related to brain function. Genetic studies, including twin studies, look at the influence of genetics and heredity on mood disorders and attempt to isolate the specific genes involved.

Clinical research studies involve studying patients themselves and their families to learn how environmental factors affect mood disorders and what treatments work best. All these areas of research have the common goal of finding new and better ways to diagnose, treat, prevent, and someday cure mood disorders.

Improving Diagnosis

One area of neuroscientific research involves a technique called brain imaging. Brain imaging uses advanced technology to examine the inner workings of the brain and pinpoint problems with the structure and function of the brain. The structure of the brain can be seen with magnetic resonance imaging (MRI). MRI is similar to an X-ray in that it gives doctors a picture of the brain, but instead of radiation, MRI uses a strong magnetic field to create the picture. Functional MRI (fMRI) is an MRI that provides information on both the structure and activity of the brain and its neurons and detects abnormalities

Magnetic resonance imaging, or MRI, is now being used in some instances to diagnose mood disorders, especially bipolar disorder.

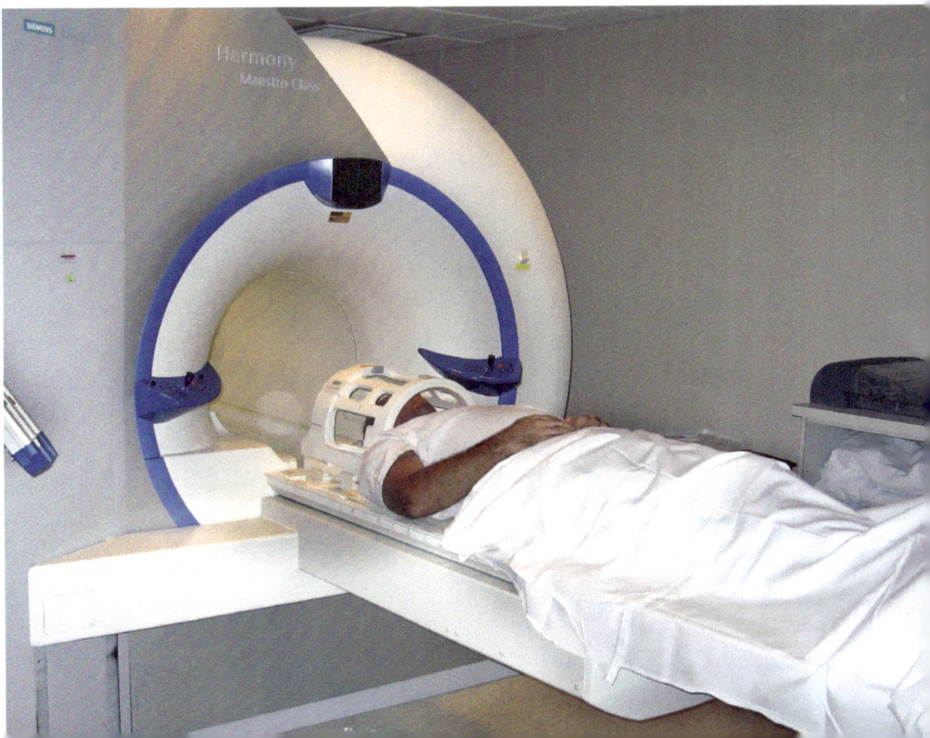

in how they work. Researchers are using these scans to study the brains of people with mood disorders and compare them to the brains of healthy people. For example, repeated MRIs were used in a 2007 study to show that the brains of children with bipolar disorder have a pattern of development that is different from healthy children and even from children with other mental illnesses such as schizophrenia, a very severe mental illness that includes hallucinations and bizarre thought patterns. Researchers hope that the information gleaned from MRIs will help with earlier diagnosis and with evaluating the effectiveness of treatment methods.

Another advanced diagnostic method that uses a magnetic field is called magnetic resonance spectrometry (MRS). MRS measures chemical compounds within the brain to provide information about the chemical changes associated with mental illnesses. Researchers at the Mayo Clinic, a renown medical center in Minnesota, are looking at MRS as a way to make diagnosing bipolar disorder easier. “The psychiatric community clearly needs a tool to help diagnose bipolar disorder,” says Dr. John Port of the Mayo Clinic. “We are hopeful that very high-field MR spectroscopy will prove helpful by identifying metabolic markers of the disease.”[29]

Genetic Research

Another focus for improving diagnosis of mood disorders is genetic research. Studies of families, twins, and adoption have long suggested that there is a genetic, or inherited, tendency toward mental illness in general and in mood disorders in particular. Traditional research into the genetics of mental illness has focused on trying to locate a single particular genetic mutation, or mistake, that could account for each kind of mental illness. Scientists now believe that it is more likely a combination of genetic factors, working with environmental influences, that are responsible for the development of mental illness. Research using newer technologies focuses on identifying which combinations of genetic variations are associated with specific illnesses. For example, in 2003, researchers at the Uni-

An Unexpected Discovery

In 2004 patients and researchers studying bipolar disorders at a psychiatric hospital in Boston made a surprising discovery when they noticed that patients undergoing brain scans for comparison with healthy brains came out of the scanning machine feeling happier than they did before the scan. When Bruce Cohen, the chief psychiatrist at the hospital, heard about it, he decided to investigate further. "I was excited but skeptical," he says. "One part of me said, 'It's unlikely.' But another part said, 'Why not?' People go in and out of depression on their own. Electromagnetic fields generated by the scanner could nudge a depressed brain back toward normal." They decided to conduct an extra experiment.

In their experiment thirty people being treated for bipolar disorder had MRI scans. Ten additional patients had "fake" scans, with no electromagnetic field. Then, fourteen healthy people had scans. Twenty-three of the bipolar patients (77 percent), which included all of those not on any medication, felt better after their scans. Only three (30 percent) of those who had fake scans and four (29 percent) of the healthy people said they felt better.

"It's a small study based on an accidental discovery," Dr. Cohen reported to the *Harvard University Gazette* in 2004. "But our results suggest that the electric fields produced by certain types of brain scans are associated with mood improvement in people with bipolar disorder." The next step will be to conduct a larger study to answer questions such as how it works and how long the effect lasts.

Quotes from William J. Cromie, "Depressed get a lift from MRI," *Harvard University Gazette*, January 22, 2004.

versity of Cambridge in England discovered that bipolar disorder and another severe mental illness called schizophrenia seem to have the same genetic defect. The defect involves the function of special nerve cells called oligodendrocytes. These cells produce myelin, the protective coating around nerve cells. In schizophrenia and bipolar disease, the oligodendrocytes do not work properly. Up until the late 1990s, most research on mental illness has focused on how messages are sent at the synapses, the space between the ends of the nerve cells. “Now,” says one researcher, “we are focusing on the oligodendrocyte and the maintenance of the myelin sheath, how the message is transmitted through the cabling [the nerve cells themselves] rather than through the synapse.”[30] The researchers hope that this knowledge will lead to quicker and more accurate diagnostic tests and new types of medications.

Another study, done at the University College in London, identified a gene on chromosome 12, named the Slynar gene, that is linked to both bipolar disorder and depression. A chromosome is a strand of genetic material that forms DNA. Chromosome 12 is the third gene found to be associated with bipolar disorder. “The next step,” says one of the researchers, “is to determine the role of the Slynar gene in the brain and how abnormalities in this gene may cause bipolar disorder. We hope our discovery will eventually lead to new treatments for depression and bipolar disorder, including possible preventive strategies, for example with drugs or even through nutritional intervention.”[31]

Help from Mice

Researchers in Texas have found that a mutation in the gene in the brain that regulates circadian rhythms may play a role in the manic phase of bipolar disorder. Circadian rhythms are the normal everyday rhythms of sleeping, waking, eating, hormone release, and body temperature. Many people with bipolar disorder also have disturbances in their circadian rhythms. The researchers found that when this gene, called the CLOCK gene, is disrupted in mice, the mice display behaviors remarkably similar to manic behaviors. “These mice look, basically in every way we can test them, like bipolar patients in the manic state,”[32] says Dr. Colleen McClung, the study leader.When the mice were given lithium, the most common treatment for bipo-

Using mice to study bipolar disorder allow researchers to learn more about the illness and the best ways to treat it.

lar disorder, their behavior stabilized. Their behavior also stabilized when a normal CLOCK gene was put back into their brains.

Being able to study manic-type behaviors in animals such as mice helps scientists learn more about the disorder in humans. "Taken together," says one of the researchers, "the whole profile of behaviors is very similar to bipolar patients when they're in a manic stage. This is really important because there hasn't been a good or complete model of human mania. This is the most complete model ever described."[33]

Transcranial Magnetic Stimulation (TMS)

One procedure that can be used in both diagnosis and treatment is Transcranial Magnetic Stimulation (TMS). TMS was originally developed as a diagnostic tool for examining brain function. Research done since the late 1990s has shown that it also holds promise for treating several kinds of mental illness, especially in patients with major depression for whom other treatment methods have not worked well.

TMS, like MRI, uses a strong magnetic field. In TMS, a powerful electromagnet is placed on the scalp over an area of the brain called the left prefrontal cortex, near the top of the forehead. This part of the brain becomes less active in depressed people. The electrical current generated by the magnet stimulates the neurons in the brain under the magnet and alters how the neurons function. From there, the effects can spread to deeper areas of the brain that are connected to the prefrontal cortex, particularly the limbic system, the center of human emotional response in the brain.

TMS has also been studied in bipolar patients. One study showed a significant decrease in manic symptoms when TMS was applied to the right prefrontal cortex. TMS remains an experimental treatment, but results are encouraging. "This is a great neuroscience tool for testing the relationship between brain and behavior," says one researcher. "We're just beginning to understand how to use it."[34]

Improving Treatment

In addition to improving diagnosis, another major area of research involves improving existing treatments for mood disorders. An important part of this is research and development of medications. Drug companies are developing new medications, as well as exploring the effectiveness of existing drugs, for treating depression and bipolar. For example, in 2006, as a result of three different studies, the U.S. Food and Drug Administration (FDA) approved the use of a drug called Wellbutrin, already approved for major depression, to treat seasonal affective disorder (SAD). It is the first drug approved for SAD. "Seasonal affective disorder can significantly impair the quality of life of patients with this condition," says Dr. Steven Galson of the FDA. "Today's approval can help patients with this condition to avoid the depressive symptoms and impaired functioning that typically affect them in the fall and winter."[35]

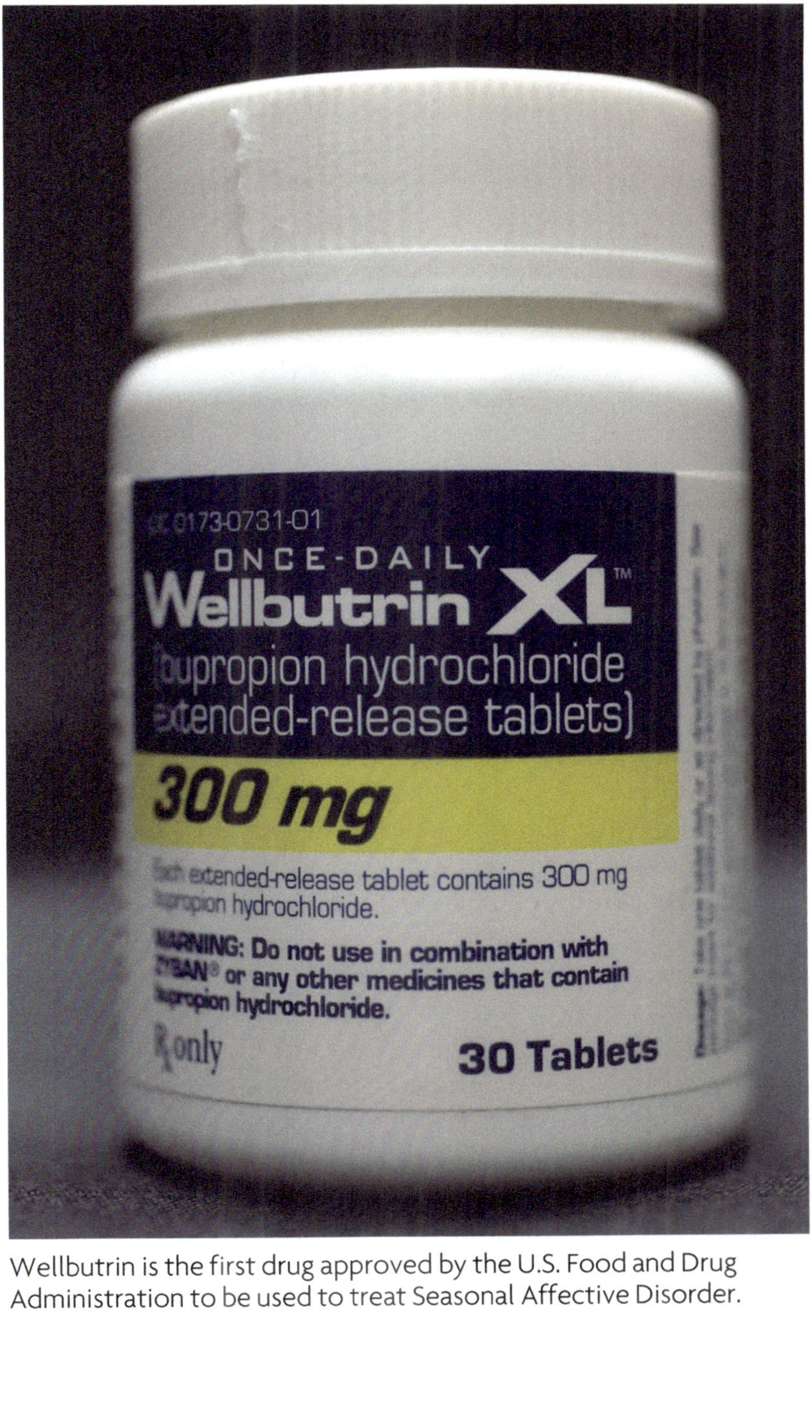

Wellbutrin is the first drug approved by the U.S. Food and Drug Administration to be used to treat Seasonal Affective Disorder.

Much work is being done on how certain drugs work in the brain to change the function of the neurons. Most antidepressants and mood stabilizers take several weeks before showing improvement in symptoms; studies are looking at specifically where in the brain the medications work, to aid in the development of more targeted drugs that may decrease the time they take to begin working. Other research is focused on diminishing the side effects of such drugs. Still other studies are examining what drugs or combinations of drugs work best in particular subtypes of depression. For example, people with a subtype of depression called atypical depression seem to respond better to MAOIs or SSRIs than to the tricyclic medications. Scientists are also working to develop new drugs for bipolar disorders and to better understand how lithium works and why it works for some patients and not for others. Knowing these things will help doctors find effective treatment strategies sooner.

Doctors are also studying how best to use medications in combination with talk therapies for depression and bipolar disorders. Some younger patients do well with cognitive-behavioral therapy alone; others need the addition of medication. In adults, psychotherapy alone is rarely enough; most need medication as well. In some patients, such as older adults and those with dysthymia, interpersonal therapy may be all that is needed. Interpersonal therapy focuses on mending dysfunctional, or impaired, personal relationships.

Learning More about ECT

In addition to studying medications, scientists continue to learn more about electroconvulsive therapy (ECT). ECT remains one of the most effective treatments for severe depression, but it usually requires several treatment sessions, and its benefits do not last over time. Researchers are studying ways to improve ECT by diminishing its side effects, increasing its effectiveness, and maintaining its benefits over a longer period of time.

One study, conducted at Columbia University and published in spring 2007, showed that an animal version of ECT can cause the growth of new nerve cells, a process called neurogenesis,

"Wake Up" Pill for Bipolar Disorder

A drug that has been used for certain kinds of sleep disorders is being studied as a possible treatment for the depressive phase of bipolar disorder. Modafinil is sometimes called the "wake-up" drug because it is used to help people with excessive daytime sleepiness caused by narcolepsy (uncontrollable falling asleep during the day) or obstructive sleep apnea, and for people whose sleep rhythms are disrupted from working night shifts. Researchers wondered if it would help bipolar patients who are excessively sleepy or fatigued during the day because of their depressive symptoms.

The initial study, completed in 2005, looked at eighty-five patients. Half were given the drug and the other half were given a placebo. None of the patients knew which pill they were taking. Forty-four percent of the patients in the study group reported improved symptoms, compared to 23 percent in the placebo group.

Dr. Mark Frye, the leader of the study, says, "There are very few treatments for the depressive phase of bipolar disorder and as a result there is an urgent need to evaluate potential new therapeutics. Mood stabilizers in general are better at treating mania than depression, but the depressive phase of the illness is far more common. We really need continued research in this area."

Quote from "'Wake-up Pill' under Study to Treat Bipolar Disorders," *Science Blog*, August 3, 2007, http://www.scienceblog.com/cms/wake-pill-under-study-treat-bipolar-disorders-13853.html.

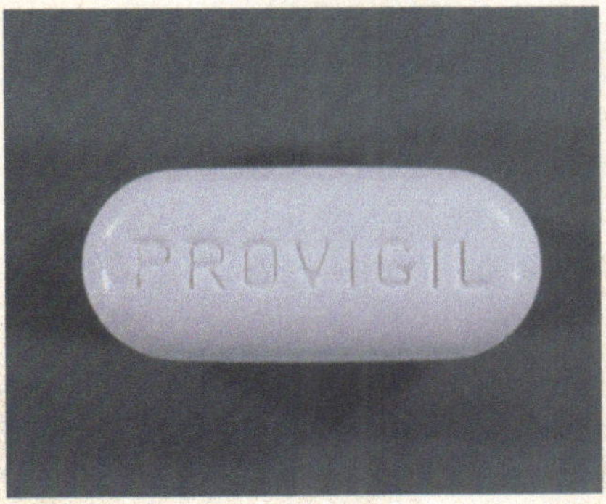

In some cases, the drug Modafinil is now being used to treat the depression phase of bipolar disorder.

in the hippocampus of the brain of adult monkeys. The hippocampus is part of the limbic system and is involved in learning and memory. In depressed people, the hippocampus has been observed to be smaller than those in healthy people. According to Dr. Tarique Perera, who led the study, "These findings support the hypothesis that ...neurogenesis is a necessary component in the mechanism of action of antidepressant treatments."[36] This means that antidepressant treatments such as ECT may help by actually increasing the number of healthy nerve cells in the brain.

Real World Studies

Clinical studies add further information to neuroscientific and genetic research. Clinical studies involve studying the development and progression of illnesses in the patients themselves. They help evaluate the reliability of a diagnostic tool, the effectiveness of a treatment plan, or the value of a prevention method by following patients over time and measuring their progress.

Traditionally, clinical studies have focused on studying only one treatment, such as a medication or a particular talk therapy. Others have focused on a very limited population of study subjects in a limited geographical area. They also tend to exclude from the study people who have other illnesses that could affect the results.

Newer studies, called "real world" studies, look at very large populations of patients, from all areas of the country. They include patients with more than one type of mental illness, with other physical illnesses, or with chemical addictions in addition to their mental illness. They involve several different treatment strategies and examine at how they work as the patients go through their normal everyday lives of home, work, school, and social functioning. These kinds of studies give a better picture of how treatment works in the kinds of patients doctors are most likely to treat.

A real world study completed in spring 2007 is called the Systematic Treatment Enhancement Program for Bipolar Dis-

Studying patients in real world situations, such as at home, work, and school, give researchers a better idea of what treatments will work best for patients as they go throughout their day.

order, or the STEP-BD study. The study included several different topics. One arm of the study showed that bipolar patients do no better when an antidepressant is added to their treatment regimen of mood stabilizing medications. In fact, manic symptoms were worse in those patients who had received both medications. These results have led many physicians to alter their medication routines for bipolar patients.

Another focus of the STEP-BD study showed that bipolar patients who receive intensive psychotherapy along with medication recover from depression faster and stay well longer than those who receive only brief periods of therapy with their medication. According to Dr. David Miklowitz, the leader of the study, "Intensive psychotherapy, when used as an adjunctive [added] treatment to medication, can significantly enhance a person's chances for recovering from depression and staying healthy over the long term. It should be considered a vital part of the effort to treat bipolar illness."[37] Research projects such as the STEP-BD are valuable in improving the treatment of mood disorders.

Mood Disorders and Sleep

One aspect of daily life that seems to be closely connected to mood disorders is sleep. Most people have experienced the tired, irritable feeling that comes from getting too little sleep. Insomnia, or the inability to fall or stay asleep for three weeks or more, has long been known to be a symptom of depression. New research is beginning to show that insomnia may, in some cases, actually trigger depression. One study concluded that people with long-term insomnia are forty times more likely to develop depression within a year than those who get enough sleep. Another study found that of teens who had experienced insomnia, about half later developed depression.

The main theory of why insomnia and depression seem so closely connected has to do with the neurotransmitter serotonin. Among other functions, serotonin regulates both mood and sleep, and the level of serotonin is low in both insomniacs and depressed people. Although it may be difficult to determine which came first, insomnia or depression, treating insomnia is usually easier. “Any intervention for sleep problems may defer the need for a ‘pound of cure’ for depression,”[38] says sleep researcher Michael Perlis.

Another sleep problem may also play a role in depression. Some people, especially those who are overweight, experience a partial obstruction of their upper air passages when they sleep. They may snore a lot and may actually stop breathing for several seconds many times during the night, a condition called obstructive sleep apnea (OSA). These constant interruptions in breathing cause the person to sleep poorly and prevent him from getting enough deep, restful sleep at night. As a result, people with OSA may experience excessive sleepiness, headaches, and irritability during the day.

A common treatment for OSA has been shown to alleviate depressive symptoms in OSA patients who also suffer from depression. Continuous Positive Airway Pressure, or CPAP, uses a special mask worn over the nose to provide a steady stream of air into the patient's upper airway, preventing the snoring and episodes of apnea. The study showed significant and long-lasting improvement in depressive symptoms when CPAP was used every night. More research is needed to determine exactly how CPAP works to help depression.

Mood Disorders and Nutrition

Another aspect of daily life related to mood disorders is nutrition and diet. Research at Harvard University suggests that certain nutrients seem to be especially effective for reducing depressive symptoms. Researchers observed that depression rates are lower in countries where fish is a large part of the diet. They used laboratory rats to experiment and found that omega-3 fatty acids, found in cold-water fish such as sardines, herring, tuna, and salmon, seem to have an effect similar to antidepressant medications. While the reason it works is not clear, one theory is that these compounds work by helping the flow of neurotransmitters in the brain. More research is needed to confirm whether or not the same results will be true in humans. "It highlights that we have some control over the things we put in our body," says the study leader, "and those things will affect how our body will function. It puts more responsibility on people to be more careful about what they put in their bodies."[39]

Fish oil has also been shown to help children with bipolar disorder, for whom adult mood stabilizers such as lithium are not very helpful. Such information could lead to an alternative treatment for children with bipolar disorder and help them avoid the unpleasant side effects of medications.

Diet-mood connection

Nutrient	Food sources	Neurotransmitter/mechanism	Proposed effect
Protein	Meat, milk, eggs, cheese, fish, beans	Dopamine, Norepinephrine	Increased alertness, concentration
Carbohydrate (CHO)	Grains, fruits, sugars	Serotonin	Increased calmness, relaxation
Calories	All foods	Reduced blood flow to the brain	Excess calories in a meal is associated with decreased alertness and concentration after the meal

Another nutritional supplement being studied as an alternative to medications is called SAMe. SAMe is a natural chemical found in all the body's cells. It plays a role in the production of serotonin and other brain chemicals that regulate mood. Many studies have already shown that SAMe can be as effective as tricyclic medications, without the side effects. A study in the mid-2000s at Massachusetts General Hospital in Boston is comparing SAMe to the newer SSRIs. "This is an important study," says one of the researchers. "If SAMe does prove to be effective, it would be a valuable alternative for people who prefer not to take regular medications."[40]

Research in the field of mental illness in general and mood disorders in particular has exploded since the 1990s. With the remarkable increase in diagnosed cases of depression, bipolar disorder, seasonal affective disorder, and other mood disorders, doctors and scientists around the world are working to find better ways to diagnose, treat, prevent, and cure these life-changing illnesses. Thanks to progress made possible by research, the future holds more promise than ever before for people with mood disorders to live full and satisfying lives.

Notes

Introduction: An Exploding Epidemic

1. Quoted in John McManamy, "Peggy's Story," *Suite 101.com*, June 22, 1999. http://www.suite101.com/article.cfm/depression/18270.
2. Quoted in McManamy, "Peggy's Story."
3. Quoted in "Understanding Mood Disorders," *Awake Magazine*, January 8, 2004. http://www.watchtower.org/e/20040108/article_02.htm.
4. Quoted in Tammy Joyner, "The Blues Can be a Workplace Burden," *The Atlanta Journal-Constitution*, July 12, 2007.

Chapter One: What Are Mood Disorders?

5. Quoted in "Scientists Identify Gene Region Linked to Severe Depression," NARSAD—The Mental Health Research Association, March7, 2007. http://www.narsad.org/news/press/rg_2007/res2007-03-08.html.
6. Prentiss Price, PhD., "Environmental Causes of Depression," All About Depression, 2004. http://www.allaboutdepression.com/cau_04.html.

Chapter Two: Types of Mood Disorders

7. Quoted in Faye Zucker and Joan E. Huebl, PsyD, *Beating Depression*. New York: Franklin Watts, 2007, p. 8.
8. Quoted in "Men and Depression," *At Health, Inc.*, NIH Publications, 2003. www.athealth.com/consumer/disorders/depressionmen.html.
9. Quoted in Zucker and Huebl, *Beating Depression*, p. 21.
10. Quoted in Joann Jovinelly, *Bipolar Disorder and Manic Depressive Illness*. New York: The Rosen Publishing Group, 2001, p. 32.
11. Quoted in Jovinelly, *Bipolar Disorder and Manic Depressive Illness*, p. 15.

Chapter Three: Diagnosis and Treatment

12. Quoted in Zucker and Huebl, *Beating Depression*, p. 54.
13. Maureen Empfield, and Nicholas Bakalar, *Understanding Teenage Depression*. New York: Holt and Company, 2007, p. 30.
14. Quoted in Judith Peacock, *Bipolar Disorder*. Mankato, MN: Life Matters Books, 2000, p. 48.
15. Quoted in Wendy Moragne, *Depression*. Brookfield, CT: Twentieth Century Books, 2001, p. 55–6.

Chapter Four: Living with Mood Disorders

16. Quoted in Joyner, "The Blues Can be a Workplace Burden."
17. Quoted in Zucker and Huebl, *Beating Depression*, p. 82.
18. Quoted in Zucker and Huebl, *Beating Depression*, p. 82–3.
19. Quoted in David Blackburn, "Caring and Sharing: Woman Starts Local Bipolar Support Group." *Messenger-Inquirer*, Owenboro, KY, April 19, 2007.
20. Empfield and Bakalar, *Understanding Teenage Depression*, pp. 113–14.
21. Quoted in Moragne, *Depression*, p. 52.
22. Quoted in Zucker and Huebl, *Beating Depression*, p. 100.
23. Quoted in Joyner, "The Blues Can be a Workplace Burden."
24. Quoted in Scott Reeves, "Disclosing Bipolar Disorder," *Forbes.com*, September 15, 2005. http://www.forbes.com/careers/2005/09/14/bipolar-disability-career-cx_sr_0915bizbasics.html.
25. Quoted in Jessica Adler, "Desire to Work Strong in Many of the Mentally Ill; Programs Exist to Help Them Achieve that Goal," July 18, 2005. http://www.pendulum.org/bp-news/archive/001726.html.
26. Sabina Morris, "Building a Career When Living With a Mood Disorder." http://akmhcweb.org/recovery/building_a_career.htm.
27. Quoted in Zucker and Huebl, *Beating Depression*, p. 94.
28. Quoted in Amy Weintraub, "Yoga: Not Just an Exercise," *Psychology Today*, November/December 2000. http://psychologytoday.com/articles/pto-20001101-000022.html.

Chapter Five: On the Horizon

29. Quoted in "Scans May Spot Bipolar Disorder," *Ajc.com*, November 30, 2004. http://www.ajc.com/health/content/shared-auto/healthnews/brai/522557.html.
30. Quoted in "Two Mental Disorders, One Genetic Defect," *Ajc.com*, September 5, 2007. http://www.ajc.com/health/content/shared-auto/healthnews/schz/514957.html.
31. Quoted in "New Gene Linked to Bipolar Disorder," NARSAD—The Mental Health Research Association, November 2, 2006. http://www.narsad.org/news/press/rg_2006/res2006-11-04.html.
32. Quoted in "Mice Provide Insight into Bipolar Disorder: UT Southwestern Scientists Find Breed with Manic Tendencies," *The Dallas Morning News*, March 20, 2007.
33. Quoted in "Circadian Rhythms Linked to Bipolar Disorder," *Ajc.com*, March 20, 2007. http://www.ajc.com/health/content/shared-auto/healthnews/bipo/602902.html.
34. Quoted in Laura Helmuth, "Boosting Brain Activity From the Outside In." http://www.sciencemag.org/cgi/content/short/292/5520/1284.
35. Quoted in "FDA Approves First Drug for Seasonal Depression," *FDA News*, June 12, 2006. http://www.fda.gov/bbs/topics/NEWS/2006/NEW01388.html.
36. Quoted in "Antidepressant Therapy Spurred New Neuron Growth in Monkeys," NARSAD—The Mental Health Research Association, May 11, 2007. http://www.narsad.org/dc/depression/featured.html.
37. Quoted in "New Study Shows Intensive Psychotherapy to Be More Effective Than Brief Therapy for Treating Bipolar Depression," NARSAD—The Mental Health Research Association, April 12, 2007. http://www.narsad.org/news/press/rg_2007/res2007-04-12.html.
38. Quoted in Karen Barrow, "Up All Night, Down All Day," *Psychology Today*, March/April, 2007. http://psychologytoday.com/rss/index.php?term=pto-20070308-000001&print=1.
39. Quoted in Alvin Powell, "Rx for Depression: 'Mangia, Mangia!'," *Harvard University Gazette*, March 3, 2005. http://www.news.harvard.edu/gazette/2005/03.03/28-eathappy.html.

40. Quoted in “Mass. General, Butler Hospitals Testing SAMe for Depression Treatment,” Massachusetts General Hospital, June 26, 2007. http://www.massgeneral.org/news/releases/062607mischoulon.html.

Glossary

amygdala: Small, almond-shaped structure in the brain, part of the limbic system, involved in emotions of fear and aggression.

antidepressant: A class of medications specifically designed to treat the symptoms of depression.

autonomic nervous system: The part of the human nervous system that controls basic functions such as heart rate, blood pressure, and sweating.

bipolar: Having two opposite extremes, or poles.

brain imaging: A method of examining the inner structures of the brain.

circadian rhythms: The natural biological cycles that govern such functions as sleep, wakefulness, and hormone secretion.

cognitive behavior therapy (CBT): A form of talk therapy that teaches patients to think about events and feelings in a more positive, healthy way.

cortisol: A hormone produced by the adrenal glands in response to stress.

cycling: The back-and-forth shifting of mood from manic to depressive in bipolar disorder.

cyclothymia: A milder but longer-lasting form of bipolar disorder in which the mood swings are less intense than in other forms of the disorder.

depression: A mood disorder characterized by deep feelings of sadness, hopelessness, and worthlessness.

DNA: The genetic material in the cells that determines what characteristics an individual living organism will have.

dopamine: A chemical neurotransmitter, produced in the brain, which has a part in the formation of emotions.

dysthymia: A milder but long-lasting form of depression.

electroconvulsive therapy (ECT): A method of treatment for depression that uses an electrical current to change the chemistry in the brain and relieve depressive symptoms.

emotion: A complex state of feeling that occurs in response to events that are meaningful in some way.

endocrine system: The system of glands in the body that secrete hormones.

endorphins: Chemicals produced in the brain in response to pain or stress that create a feeling of well-being and raise the pain threshold.

flight of ideas: The rapid speech and frequent changes of thought that are sometimes seen in the manic phase of bipolar disorder.

genes: The basic unit of heredity; segments of DNA that carry the instructions for expression of characteristics.

genome: The entire array of genes for a particular living organism.

hippocampus: The part of the limbic system in the brain responsible for making and storing memory.

hormones: Chemicals made by the endocrine glands that affect the function of other organs that are receptive to them.

hypersomnia: Excessive sleeping.

hypnosis: A therapeutic technique that uses focused relaxation to increase suggestibility and create healthier ways of thinking.

hypomania: A mild form of mania characterized by elevated mood, energy, and creativity.

hypothalamus: The part of the brain that controls many of the functions of the body through its effects on the endocrine and autonomic nervous systems.

insomnia: The inability to fall asleep or stay asleep over a period of days or weeks.

limbic system: The set of structures in the brain that affect emotional response.

lithium: A naturally-occurring mood-stabilizing medication effective for treating the symptoms of bipolar disorder.

magnetic resonance imaging (MRI): A technique of brain imaging that uses a powerful magnetic field to create a picture of the structures of the brain.

magnetic resonance spectrometry: A technique for examining chemical compounds in the brain that relate to emotion and mood.

mania: The phase of bipolar disorder that is characterized by, among other symptoms, over-elevated mood, hyperactivity, rapid speech, and sometimes irritability or aggression.

melatonin: A hormone produced in the brain that is elevated during periods of darkness and affects sleep and other circadian rhythms.

monoamine oxidase inhibitor (MAOI): An early class of antidepressant medications.

mood: A prolonged state of emotion or combination of emotions that affects the way a person views the world.

mood stabilizer: A class of medications that works to stabilize mood fluctuations in bipolar disorder.

myelin: The protective sheath, or coating, around nerve cells.

neuroscience: The branch of science that has to do with the physiological and chemical workings of the brain and nervous system.

neurotransmitters: Chemicals produced in the brain that carry electrical impulses from one nerve cell to the next.

norepinephrine: A neurotransmitter that is involved with emotional response.

obstructive sleep apnea: A condition that causes partial blockage of the upper airways during sleep, causing snoring and short periods of apnea, or not breathing.

oligodendrocytes: Specialized nerve cells that produce myelin.

phototherapy: A method for treating seasonal affective disorder that uses high-intensity light.

pituitary: A pea-sized gland in the brain that sends hormonal messages to the other endocrine glands in response to instructions from the hypothalamus.

postpartum depression: A type of depressive disorder that occurs after childbirth.

psychiatrist: A physician who specializes in the treatment of mental illnesses.

psychological: Related to the function of the mind.

psychologist: A highly trained mental health professional who diagnoses and treats mental disorders.

psychosis: A very severe symptom of mental illness in which the person loses touch with reality and may have hallucinations or delusions.

psychotherapy: A method of treating mental or emotional disorders in which a person or group of people discuss issues, concerns, and thoughts with a trained therapist.

schizophrenia: One of the most severe forms of mental illness that includes hallucinations, delusional thinking, and inability to recognize what is real.

seasonal affective disorder (SAD): A depressive disorder in which symptoms appear during the fall and winter months.

selective serotonin reuptake inhibitor (SSRI): A class of medications used to treat symptoms of depression.

serotonin: A neurotransmitter that plays a role in emotional responses.

stigma: The negative or shameful character attached to mental illness.

subconscious: The part of the mind's mental processes of which a person is not aware.

suicide: The act of taking one's own life.

synapse: The space between neurons across which electrical impulses are sent.

transcranial magnetic stimulation (TMS): A diagnostic and treatment method that uses a magnetic field to alter the function of the nerve cells in the brain to relieve symptoms of mental disorders.

tricyclic: A class of medications used to treat depressive disorders.

unipolar: Having symptoms at only one end, or pole, of the range of moods.

Organizations to Contact

American Academy of Child and Adolescent Psychiatry

3615 Wisconsin Avenue NW
Washington, DC 20016
(202) 966-7300
www.aacap.org

A national professional medical association dedicated to treating and improving the quality of life for children, adolescents, and families affected by mental, behavioral, or developmental disorders.

American Psychiatric Association

1000 Wilson Blvd, Suite 1825
Arlington, VA 22209
(703) 907-7300
www.psych.org

An organization of more than 35,000 U.S. and international physicians who work together to ensure humane care and effective treatment for all people with mental disorders.

Depression and Bipolar Support Alliance

730 North Franklin Street, Suite 501
Chicago, IL 60610
(800) 826-3632
www.dbsalliance.org

A patient-driven national organization focusing on bipolar and depressive illnesses that provides education for the public and supports research.

Mental Health America

2000 N. Beauregard Street, 6th Floor
Alexandria, VA 22311
(703) 684-7722
www.nmha.org

A nonprofit organization of people who have experienced or are recovering from mental illness, whose goals are to promote mental health, provide education and awareness to the general public, support research, and to make sure all patients have access to adequate mental health care and support.

National Alliance for the Mentally Ill

Colonial Place Three
2107 Wilson Boulevard, Third Floor
Arlington, VA 22201
(800) 950-6264
www.nami.org

A grassroots support and advocacy organization dedicated to improving the lives of patients, families, and friends of those with mental illnesses.

National Institute of Mental Health

6001 Executive Blvd, Room 8148, MSC 9663
Bethesda, MD 20892-9663
(866) 615-6464
www.nimh.nih.gov

An agency of the federal government dedicated to research focused on the understanding, treatment, and prevention of mental disorders and the promotion of mental health.

For More Information

Books

Maureen Empfield, M.D. and Nicholas Bakalar, *Understanding Teenage Depression*. New York: Henry Holt and Company, 2001. A very comprehensive guide to diagnosis, treatment, and management of depression. Good for older teens, young adults, and parents.

Joann Jovinelly, *Bipolar Disorder and Manic-Depressive Illness*. New York: The Rosen Publishing Group, 2001. Thorough, interesting, and easy to read coverage of all aspects of living with bipolar disorder.

Wendy Moragne, *Depression*. Brookfield, CT: Twenty-first Century Books, 2001. Excellent resource about depression for teens.

Judith Peacock, *Bipolar Disorder*. Mankato, MN: Life Matters, 2000. Easy to read and fully illustrated book about bipolar disorder, good for middle schoolers.

Kathleen Winkler, *Teens, Depression, and the Blues*. Berkeley Heights, NJ: Enslow Publishers, 2000. Thorough coverage of depression in teens, with a chapter about suicide.

Faye Zucker and Joan E. Huebl, PsyD, *Beating Depression*. New York: Franklin Watts, 2007. Up-to-date and well-illustrated book about teenage depression.

Web Sites

All About Depression (www.allaboutdepression.com). Thorough site with lots of information about depression.

KidsHealth.org (www.kidshealth.org). Fun and kid-friendly site that provides information for children about all aspects of their physical and mental health.

McMan's Depression and Bipolar Web (www.mcmanweb.com). Writer and recovering bipolar patient John McManamy's site dedicated to helping people manage their bipolar or depressive disorder.

NARSAD, the Mental Health Research Association (www.narsad.org). Informative site about all kinds of mental health issues, with emphasis on research support and education.

Pendulum.org (www.pendulum.org). An educational, entertaining, and very comprehensive site dedicated to bipolar disorder, with interesting content, both serious and humorous.

Index

Acupuncture, 26
Adrenal glands, 26, 27, 28
Adrenalin, 23
Aerobic exercise, 79–80
Affective disorders. *See* Mood disorders
Aggression, 23, 25, 39, 43
Agitation, 39, 42
Amygdala, 24
Ancient Greeks, 19
Anger, 14, 16, 25, 39, 42, 43
Antidepressant medications, 58–60
See also individual medications
Anxiety, 16, 39, 41, 71
Anxiety disorders, 60
Attention-getting behavior, 33
Atypical depression, 90
Autonomic nervous system, 24

Beck Depression Inventory, 54
Bedlam Lunatic Asylum, *19*
Behavioral component, of emotions, 16
Biological factors, 18, 28
Bipolar disorders, *44*
  characteristics, 14
  cycling of symptoms, 47–48, *47*
  degrees of, 46–47
  family study, 22–23
  fish oil treatment, 95
  heredity factor, 21, 22
  link with seasonal affective disorder, 40
  medications for, 60–62, 91
  mice research studies, 86–87, *87*
  risk factors, 30
  support groups, 67–68
  TMS treatment, 88
  Types I and II, 47, 48
  work-related challenges, 74
  See also Cyclothymia; Hypomania; Mania; Rapid cycling (bipolar disorder); Ultra-rapid cycling (bipolar disorder)
Bipolar NOS (not otherwise specified), 46–47
Birth defects, 61
"Black bile" (melancholia), 19
Blood pressure, 12, 29
Boston University School of Medicine, 80
Brain
  amygdala, 24
  endorphins, 26
  hippocampus/temporal lobes, 24
  limbic system, 23–24
  mood stabilizer effectiveness, 90
  MRI studies, 84, 85
  MRS studies, 85
  temporal lobes, 24
  Transcranial Magnetic Stimulation, 87–88
  See also Hypothalamus; Neurotransmitters

carbamazepine (Tegretol), 62
Carroll Rating Scale, 54
Center for Mental Health Services, 10
Center for Preventive Cardiology (University of Maryland), 29
Childbirth. *See* Postpartum depression
Children
  depression, 18, 36–38
  mental health inventories, 54
  misdiagnosis of depression, 37
  suicide rate, 33
  support from friends, 72
  teacher support, 73
Chromosomes, 22
Circadian rhythm, 40
CLOCK gene, 86–87
Cognitive behavior therapy (CBT), 56, 80–81
  See also Beck Depression Inventory
Cohen, Bruce, 85
Confidence, 16
Confusion, 39, 42, 62
Cortisol, 28, 29, 78
Crying spells, 32, 39, 41
Cutting (self-mutilation), 26, 33
Cyclothymia, 46, 62

Depakote (valproate), 62
Depression
  age factor, 10
  antidepressant medications, 58–60
  vs "the blues," 31–33, *32*
  in children/teens, 36–38, *37*
  consequences of, 33
  DSM-IV-TR definition, 34
  ECT, effectiveness of, 63, 90, 92
  in elderly, 36
  emotional/physical symptoms, *9*, 34
  exercise benefits, 79–80
  female factors, 18, 20–21, *20*
  friends, support from, 72
  heredity factor, 21–23, *22*
  historical terminology, 19
  influences on life, 31–33
  vs. medical problems, 36
  in men, 34–36, *35*
  pet therapy, 71
  postpartum depression, 8
  risk factors, 30
  school support, 72–73
  SSRIs for, 58–60, 90, 96
  work support, 73–75
  See also Atypical depression; Major depression; Serotonin
desipramine (Norpramin), 59–60
Diagnosing mood disorders
  mental health inventories, 54
  physical causes, ruling out of, 52–53
  psychiatric interview, 50–52
Diagnostic and Statistical Manual of Mental Disorders-IV-TR (DSM-IV-TR)
  bipolar NOS (definition), 47
  depression (definition), 34
  mania (definition), 34
Dietary supplements, 77, 96
Disgust, 16
Dizziness, 60
DNA, 21, 22

Dopamine, 25–26, 27, 40
Dry mouth, 60
Dysthymia, 38–39, 90

Elderly people
depression, 10, 36
mental health inventory, 53
Electroconvulsive therapy (ECT), 62–63, 90
Emotional Support Animals, 71
Emotions
behavioral component, 16
complexity/variety, 15–16
hypothalamus, 24
memory, 24
See also individual emotions
Empty nest syndrome, 21
Endocrine system, 26–28, *27*
Endorphins, 26, 29
Environmental factors, 18, 28
Euphoria, 43
Exercise, 79–80
Exorcism of evil spirits, 19
Expressed emotion (EE), 56

Families
bipolar studies, 22–23
dealing with consequences, 68–71
disorder tendencies, 68
expressed emotion (EE), 56
feelings of helplessness, 69–70, *69*
mood disorder therapy, 57–58
need for supportive attitudes, 69
sibling struggles, 70
See also Twins
Fear, 16, 23, 24, 26, 39, 41
Females
dietary supplements, 77
estrogen, 26–27
masking of symptoms, 35
ovaries, 26
prevalence of mood disorders, 10, 18, 34, 38
risk factors, 19–21
suicide, 35–36
See also Postpartum depression
"Fight or flight" response, 23
Fish oil treatment, 95
Food and Drug Administration (FDA), 60, 88
Food cravings, 39, 41
Frye, Mark, 91
Functional magnetic resonance imaging (fMRI), of brains, 83–84

Gabapentin, 62
Galson, Steven, 88
Gamma-aminobutyric acid (GABA), 80
Genetics
bipolar disorder, 21
CLOCK gene, 85–87
depression, 21–22
research studies, 22, 82, 84–87
Slynar gene, 86
See also Heredity; Twins
Greeks, ancient, 19
Grief, 11, 16
Group therapy, 56
Guilt, 38, 39, 41, 69, 70, 74

Hallucinations
mania, 45
postpartum depression, 42
Hamilton Depression Scale, 54
Hand tremors, 61

Happiness, 16, 36, 68, 72, 85
Harvard Medical School, 11
Hate, 16
Headaches
  anxiety, 16
  depression, 34
  light therapy, side effect, 64
  obstructive sleep apnea, 92
  postpartum depression, 39, 41
  SSRIs, side effect, 59, 60
Hearing voices, 45
Helplessness, 31, 41, 70
Heredity
  bipolar disorder, 21, 23
  depression, 21–23
  See also Genetics; Twins
High-risk behavior, 33
Hippocampus/temporal lobes, 24
Hippocrates, 19
History of mood disorders, 19
Hopelessness, 14, 16, 34
Hormones, 26–28, 43
Hostility, 14, 38, 42
Hotlines, 33
"Humors" of body, 19
Hypersomnia, 35
Hyperventilation, 39, 41–42
Hypnosis, 77, 79
Hypomania, 45–47, 61, 75
Hypothalamus, 23–24
  endocrine system, 27–28
  endorphins, 26
  neurotransmitters, 27
  pituitary gland, 27
Hypothyroidism, 61

imipramine (Tofranil), 59–60
Indifference, 39, 42
Insomnia, 34, 64, 94
Inventory for Depressive Symptomology, 54
Irritability
  light therapy, side effect, 64
  mania, 39, 43, 45
  men, 35
  obstructive sleep apnea, 94
  postpartum depression, 41
  teens, 38
isocarboxazid (Marplan), 58
Isolation, 9, 14, 65

Jaeger, Ellyn, 11
Jealousy, 16

Kidney disease, 61

Lamotrigine, 62
Laughing, 26, 29
Levinson, Douglas, 22
Light therapy, for SAD, 63–64, *63*
Limbic system
  amygdala, 24
  autonomic nervous system, 24
  hippocampus/temporal lobes, 24
  hypothalamus, 23–24
Lithium, 61, 62, 86, 90, 95
Loneliness, 14
Lunatic asylums, 19

Magnetic resonance imaging (MRI), 83–84, 83, 85
Magnetic resonance spectrometry (MRS), 84
Major depression, 32, 34, 39, 42
Males
  risk factors, 19–20, 21
  testosterone, 26–27
Mania, 31, 43–45
  DSM-IV definition, 45
  "flight of ideas," 44

hearing voices, 45
mice studies, 86–87
symptoms, 39
Valproate, 62
See also Bipolar disorders; Lithium
MAOIs. See Monoamine oxidase inhibitors (MAOIs)
Mayo Clinic, 84
McClung, Colleen, 86
Medications
antidepressants, 58–60
bipolar disorders, 60–62, 91
monoamine oxidase inhibitors, 60–61
SSRIs, 58–60, 90, 96
with talk therapy, 55
tricyclic antidepressants, 58, 59–60
See also individual medications
Melancholia ("black bile"), 19
Melatonin, 40
Memory loss, 24
Men
depression, 34–36
substance abuse, 35
suicide, 35–36
Menopause, 21
Menstrual cycles, 21
Mental Health America, 11
Mental illness
behavioral vs. physical symptoms, 66
biochemical causes, 23
historical terminology, 19
stigma of, 36, 65–67
Miklowitz, David J., 74
Miller, Michael, 29
Mind-body connection, 16
Modafinil ("wake-up" drug), 91, *91*
Monoamine oxidase inhibitors (MAOIs), 60–61
Montgomery and Asberg Depression Rating Scale, 54
Mood disorders
age/onset, 10, 21
bipolar vs. unipolar, 31
causes, 14, 18
and emotions, *17*
gaining knowledge about, 67–68
heredity factor, 21–22
mental health inventories, 54
nondiscrimination factor, 10–11
nutritional component, 95–96
and physical problems, *12*
possible signs of, *50*,
risk factors, 18, 20–21
sleep problems, 94–95
symptom management, 75–77, *76*
types (chart), 39
See also Bipolar disorders; Depression; Major depression; Mania
Mood stabilizers
combined with antidepressants, 61
for bipolar disorder, 60–62
mechanism of action, 60–61

National Institute of Mental Health (NIMH), 9, 11
Neuroscientific studies, 82
Neurotransmitters, *25*
dopamine, 25–26, 27, 40
gamma-aminobutyric acid (GABA), 80
mood stabilizers, action, 60
norepinephrine, 25

serotonin, 25–26
Norepinephrine, 25, 27, 59, 60
North Jersey Friendship House, 74
Nutrition and mood disorders, 77, 95–96

Obsessive-compulsive disorder (OCD), 60
Obstructive sleep apnea (OSA), 91
O'Connor, Sinead, *15*
Ovaries, 26

Pancreas, 26
Paxil (paroxetine), 59, *59*, 60
Perera, Tarique, 92
Pet therapy, 71, *71*
phenelzine (Nardil), 58
Pituitary gland, 26–27
Pleasurable activities, 26
Postpartum depression, *41*
causes, 43
crying spells, 41
defined, 40
diagnosis, 54
forms of, 41–42
symptoms, 39
Vitamin B12, 54
Pregnancy, 21, 42, 61
Price, Prentiss, 30
Prozac (fluoxetine), 59, *59*, 60
Psychiatrists, 38, 50–52, 53
Psychologists, 38, 53
Psychotherapy, 56
Psychotic behavior, 45, 46

Rapid cycling (bipolar disorder), 47, 48, 61, 62
Reckless behavior, 35
Research studies
Boston University, School of Medicine, 80
brain imaging, 83–84
cortisol, 28
depression of elderly, 10
environmental factors, 83
expressed emotion (EE), 57
family bipolar/depression, 22–23
genetics, 22, 82, 84–86, 84–87
Harvard Medical School, 11, 28
mice bipolar studies, 86–87
neurosciences, 82
neurotransmitters, 23, 80
nutrition, 95–96
postpartum depression, 43
real world studies, 92–94, *93*
St. John's wort herb, 77
Stanford University, School of Medicine, 22
Transcranial Magnetic Stimulation, 87–88
twin studies, 21–22
University College, London, 86
Resentment, 39, 42, 57, 70
Risk factors
age, 21
gender, 19–20
heredity, 21–22
See also Biological factors; Environmental factors; Stress
Running away, 33

Sadness, 14, 16, 31, 33, 39, 41
SAMe supplement, 96
Seasonal affective disorder (SAD)
geographic concentration, 40
light therapy treatment, 63–64

symptoms, 39, 40
Wellbutrin treatment, 88–89
Selective serotonin reuptake inhibitors (SSRIs), 58–60, *59*, 90, 96
Self-mutilation, 31
Serotonin
MAOIs, action, 59
mechanics of action, 25–27
seasonal affective disorder, 40
St. John's wort therapy, 77
tricyclics, action, 60
sertraline (Zoloft), 59, 60
Side effects
carbamazepine, 62
electroconvulsive therapy, 62
light therapy, 64
lithium, 61
MAOIs, 59
SSRIs, 60
tricyclics, 60
Valproate, 62
Sleep problems
insomnia, 34, 64, 94
mania, 44
and mood disorders, 94–95
narcolepsy, 91
obstructive sleep apnea, 91
postpartum depression, 41
See also Modafinil ("wake-up" drug)
Slynar gene, 86
"Snake pits" (lunatic asylums), 19
Somatic (physical) component, of emotions, 16
Spirits, exorcism of, 19
Spivack, Mala, 74
SSRIs. See Selective serotonin reuptake inhibitors (SSRIs)
St. John's wort herb, 77
Stanford University School of Medicine, 22
Stevens-Johnson Syndrome, 62
Stomachaches, 34
Stress
effect on mood, 10, 13, 28–30
endorphins, 26
family relations, 68, 70
neurotransmitters, 25
postpartum depression, 43
reduction methods, 78
women vs. men, 20
See also Cortisol
Substance abuse, 33, 35, 44
Suicide hotlines, 33
Suicide/suicidal thoughts
children/teens, 33
from depression/bipolar disorder, 14–15
ECT, effectiveness of, 63
elderly people, 36
mania, 45
SSRIs, possible side effect, 60
thoughts about, 15
warning signs, 33
Support groups, 67–68, *67*, 74–75

Talk therapies, 55–56, *55*
Teens
depression, 36–38
mania, 44–45
mental health inventories, 54
suicide rate, 33
support from friends, 72
teacher support, 73
Tegretol (carbamazepine), 61, *61*, 62
Temporal lobes, 24
Testosterone, 26–27

Thyroid gland, 26
Topiramate, 62
Transcranial Magnetic Stimulation (TMS), 87–88
tranylcypromine (Parnate), 58
Treating mood disorders
  antidepressant medications, 58–60
  bipolar medications, 60–62
  dietary supplements, 77, 95–96
  electroconvulsive therapy, 62–63
  exercise, 79–80
  family therapy, 57–58
  group therapy, 56
  hypnosis, 77, 79
  light therapy for SAD, 63–64
  patient compliance issues, 75
  pet therapy, 71
  St. John's wort herb, 77
  talk therapies, 55–56
  yoga, 80–81
Trephination (drilling skull), 19
Tricyclic antidepressants, 58, 59–60
Twins
  depression studies, 21–22, 23
  dysthymia studies, 38

Ultra-rapid cycling (bipolar disorder), 48
Unipolar mood disorders, 31, 39
  See also Depression; Dysthymia; Seasonal affective disorder (SAD)

valproate (Depakote), 62
Vitamin supplements, 77

Weight loss/gain, 34, 40, 60
Wellbutrin, 88–89, *89*
Work Adjustment Employment Support program, 74–75
Worthlessness, 14

Yoga, 80–81, *80*

Zoloft (sertraline), 59, *59*, 60
Zung Self-Rating Depression Scale, 54

Picture Credits

Cover: Image copyright Niserin, 2008. Used under license from Shutterstock.com
AP Images, 15, 44, 55
Altrendo images/Altrendo/Getty Images, 87
Custom Medical Stock Photo, Inc. Reproduced by Permission, 22, 61, 83, 91
Christopher Furlong/Getty Images News/Getty Images, 63
Gale, a part of Cengage Learning, 25, 27, 39, 95
Hulton Archive/Getty Images, 19
Image copyright Geom, 2008. Used under license from Shutterstock.com, 93
© 2008/Jupiterimages, 12, 20, 32, 35, 41, 47, 50, 71, 73, 76
Zigy Kaluzny/Stone/Getty Images, 55
Carol Kohen/Riser/Getty Images, 66
Ron Krisel/Workbook Stock Images/Jupiterimages, 9
Edward McCain/Workbook Stock/Jupiterimages, 52
Jonathan Nourok/Stone/Getty Images, 59
Photolibrary.com/Jupiterimages, 69
Joe Raedle/Getty Images News/Getty Images, 89
Claudia Rehm/Westend61/Jupiterimages, 37
Benjamin Rondel Photography/Workbook Stock/Jupiterimages, 17
David Harry Stewart/Stone/Getty Images, 67
James Wvinner/Photo Researchers, Inc., 80

About the Author

Lizabeth Peak received her Bachelor of Science in Nursing from the University of Florida in 1978 and her Bachelor of Secondary Education from Southwest Missouri State University in 1991. She currently works full time as a surgical nurse, specializing in general and vascular surgery.

Lizabeth has published both fiction and nonfiction for adults and children. She especially enjoys writing about history, biography, and medical topics. She lives in Springfield, Missouri, with her two daughters, Rebecca and Wendy, two dogs, two cats, five birds, and a python. When she is not working or writing, she enjoys reading, hiking, and St. Louis Cardinals baseball.